MW01515592

Forever Loved

Melissa Heepke-Simmons

Copyright © 2015 Melissa Heepke-Simmons
Forever Loved is a fictional work. Any character names, places, incidents
and/or events are to be considered a result of the author's imagination
and should be thought of as completely fictional. Any resemblance to
people, either living or dead, or any places depicted in this story are
entirely coincidental.

All rights reserved.

ISBN: 1517001064
ISBN-13: 9781517001063

Library of Congress Control Number: 2015919399
CreateSpace Independent Publishing Platform
North Charleston, South Carolina

This book is dedicated to the people who inspired me in life...and death.

To Andy, who planted an idea in my head during our years together. At times, he knew me better than I knew myself. His abrupt departure from my world gave me the motivation to make his dreams mine.

I also dedicate this book to my dad, who recently lost a tough battle and whose face I can no longer see. With the pride in his eyes, he showed me, in his final days, how much my writing meant to him. For that alone, I am forever grateful.

I miss and love them both more than words can say!

Acknowledgments

I would like to thank everyone who assisted with the creation of this work.

A special thank-you to Ginger Heepke, my mom, who so willingly and thoroughly proofread my initial manuscript, as well as guided me through the editing process at times.

To my daughter-in-law, Jennifer Simmons, I extend a heartfelt thank-you for using your wonderful, imaginative talent to create the book's cover art.

I would also like to recognize the patience and understanding of numerous friends and family members during the creation of this work.

In addition, I would like to take a moment to acknowledge the professionals at CreateSpace for their guidance and consideration during this project.

Starting over was all Cassie Malone could do, now that the man of her dreams, her one true love, had been ripped from her life. The middle-aged widow felt that all she could do was sit and think about the days gone by. Cassie lived a hard life before Thad, and tears began to flow as she realized that, once again, she had to learn to live without him.

Cassie's initial thoughts were of her years in the orphanage. She recalled how frightening life could be, and she remembered how hard she had worked to be strong—not allowing anyone to share that part of herself that she knew could be hurt. She had to learn not to give trust freely. As an orphan, she had actually found it essential to survive her childhood. She had stopped wishing for a family by the time she was ten.

She often confided in an imaginary friend. Larry had been such a vital part of her childhood. As part of her daily routine, she would sneak away just to talk with him. He was her one true friend—her confidant. Cassie had shared with him her dreams and strongest desires. Larry was the one "person" who would never betray her because he was a part of her.

Cassie had a fondness for the arts, but the nuns in the orphanage encouraged her to put her creativity to the side and pursue a real job when she turned eighteen and joined the real world. So that was exactly what she did. With the help of Tim, a police officer who had been a volunteer at the orphanage during her years growing up, she found a job in the real world. As a result, Cassie stifled her creativity.

The nuns convinced her to be realistic because they *saw* that she had a vivid imagination—something often found in creative people.

"You can't make money doing such frivolous work, child," Sister Anna had instructed her.

"They are just pipe dreams. You know better than that. It's a tough world out there, and you are going to have to put those ideas aside and be realistic, Cassie," Sister Catherine had concluded.

The conversations had always seemed to be the same, and one of the nuns would always complete the other's sentence, as if they were reading directly from a script.

She had spent much of her time alone, after an automobile accident had left her orphaned as an infant. Cassie had always managed very well on her own. But she had known that something was missing. Cassie hadn't felt loved in so many years and honestly wondered if it would ever happen for her.

"I'm a strong woman, and love is for the weak minded," she had reminded her younger self. Truth be told, it made for a rather lonely existence for her—until the day Thad came into her life.

During his younger years, as a confirmed bachelor, Thad had often taken long hauls—especially over the weekends. Since he had grown up an only child without knowing a man to call dad, Thad Malone had learned to live with no one in his life, especially after losing his mother. Cassie quickly became a welcomed change from the life he had grown accustomed to as a young man.

$\mathcal{N}$ow Cassie recalled the day her life began to take on a new direction. It happened early morning, just before daybreak. The thought made her smile. She had just gotten off work from her night shift. But then her car broke down, and she found herself stranded along a remote stretch of highway.

She was standing, helplessly alongside the road when the sound of a diesel engine began to give her a bit of hope. Unsure whether she really would want help from a stranger, Cassie realized she had little choice. It was miles to the nearest payphone, and she was thoroughly exhausted.

Though Thad had known it would surely make him late with his delivery, he stopped to come to her rescue.

He waited by her side until the tow truck arrived and then continued on with his scheduled haul. For the next several months, Cassie and Thad had spoken daily. Whenever he couldn't be by her side, they would spend time on the phone during the early evening, usually while he waited at the terminal for his truck to be loaded.

Cassie had quickly learned that her smile could melt his heart from a thousand miles away, and didn't hesitate to try.

She realized just how much he loved her—every time she looked into Thad's baby-blue eyes. They reminded her of a cool summer sky, enhanced by the twinkle of a brilliantly lit star. They were beautiful because he was beautiful. His appearance did not stand out in a crowd. But when Cassie looked into his soul she saw immense beauty, realizing right away that he was the man of her dreams.

One particular morning, a year after meeting Thad, Cassie dragged herself out of her car and up the walk to her door. At times her job made her feel like a saint; at other times, it made her feel as though she had been tied to a stake and then left on a busy railroad track to be run over repeatedly by a speeding locomotive. This day had been the latter—an exceptionally difficult night at work, and the scarceness of her favorite coworker, Tim, had not lessened her burden.

Cassie paused on her front stoop. She could barely see the dimly lit room through the closed blinds. But something was different from when she'd left. She fumbled through her purse for the bottle of pepper spray that Thad had insisted she carry after they had met along that desolate roadway just one year before.

Nervous, Cassie pushed open the door—and to her surprise, the sound of softly playing music met her ears. She felt an immediate sense of security and warmth. The past year had been about learning to live with emotions unfamiliar to her younger self. And this moment was about to become a sweet memory—something she had not encountered often in her twenty-two years.

Cassie let up her grip on the pepper spray—which had begun to imprint in her tightly clasped fist—when she saw a trail of rose petals along the floor. At this point, Cassie felt compelled to follow faint sounds of brass instrumental music through the foyer and down the hall.

As she entered the kitchen, she noticed a covered plate, swaddled by a white satin ribbon, resting on the table. The elegantly set table included one single red rose in the center along with a heart-shaped picture frame. Inside the frame was a picture of the man she had grown to love and admire—the same man who had come to her rescue exactly one year before. Next to the picture was a steaming-hot plate of eggs Benedict and French toast, her two favorite breakfast foods. While it was little consolation for his absence, Cassie appreciated the sentiment. Grinning, she sat and ate.

Thad had grown to know her so well, and he made no secret that it was his lot in life to make her smile any way he could—and yet he had forced her to spend this weekend without him. While Cassie had tried to hide her disappointment, her heart seemed to break a little. She had been looking forward to this day for a while. It marked the one-year anniversary of their meeting. But she had realized that she would be spending it without Thad, the one person with whom she longed to be. She was sad to think that he might find a few extra dollars more important than her feelings.

If she'd had to guess, she would have attributed it all to her wonderful neighbor and landlord, who had become almost like a mother to her when she had first rented the house four years before. Cassie had confided in Tammy about her sadness the day before.

"I know this may sound a little selfish and maybe even a bit immature, but I really had hoped to spend the anniversary of our first year together with Thad," Cassie confessed.

"You are not being selfish, but I am sure that he would be here with you if there were any way possible, sweetie," Tammy had replied, in an effort to raise the young girl's spirits.

With those words, Cassie had realized that Tammy and Thad must have spoken before he left. Her initial thought, when she had found the rose petals and breakfast, was that, Tammy had shared Cassie's feelings with

Thad, who in turn had asked her to make Cassie feel less alone.

Just as she was emptying her plate, the roar of a diesel engine made Cassie jump from her chair and race to the front of her house. It sounded like something had appeared from what seemed to be nowhere and stopped right in front of her house.

Now, in her living room, Cassie was so tired after the exhausting night of crises at work that she really hadn't taken time to process the events of this morning—the rose petals, the breakfast.

Once again she peeked through the pulled shades, though this time she was on the inside peeking out, and Cassie witnessed an unexpected and startling sight. The flashing red-and-blue lights of the police escort were yet another indication that something was not normal. She decided that a closer look was now warranted. She opened the door and blinked—her eyesight had become hindered by the sun rising above the illegally parked semi in front of her somewhat secluded home.

As she walked closer to the tractor trailer, her focus became clearer. She could now see that it was Thad's tractor sitting there. But he was supposed to be out on the East Coast for another three days. It had saddened her when he had given her the news just days before: "I am sorry, love, but there is a top-dollar load that needs to be in Boston at 8:00 a.m. Monday morning, leaving from Missouri on Friday night. I was lucky to get this haul, and I just can't pass it up. Please understand that I would rather be with you, but I have to go."

But that was not the case, and Cassie was beginning to put the pieces of the puzzle together. The conspiracy had gone much deeper than she could have ever imagined.

Now that the sun had risen slightly higher, Cassie could make out a new paint job on Thad's trailer: a large, beautifully detailed red rose surrounded by a brightly illuminated heart. The image was so big that it could have been seen from anywhere within view of the trailer. Upon further inspection, she realized that a banner fluttered over the top of the flower. It read: PLEASE JOIN ME ON THE LONG HAUL.

Cassie moved her focus toward the bottom of the enormous painted rose, down to the tip of the heart: WILL YOU MARRY ME, CASSIE?

No sooner had she finished reading the words than an arm reached around from behind her, handing her yet another magnificent red rose. But this rose had something attached to its stem: a white satin bag, which she had initially mistaken for a tacky hang tag. Cassie realized that she was wrong, and she felt a hard, round object enclosed in the bag.

She took the rose from Thad's hand, and he got down on one knee before her.

"Would you?" was all he said.

She almost laughed. Cassie had learned to appreciate his modus operandi. During what was undoubtedly the most romantic moment of her life, the person responsible for an unforgettably ecstatic round of emotion had only uttered two words: "Would you?" Yet he had said so much. Thad had once again allowed images to do his talking for him

Tears formed in the corners of her eyes. "Absolutely yes!" she replied without a moment's hesitation.

Tim exited the driver's seat of the police car that had escorted Thad to her home and offered his congratulations. "I had such a difficult time keeping from spoiling this surprise, Cassie," Tim said. They had worked together since that very first day, when she had turned eighteen and left the orphanage. He had been such a big part of her life, and she was happy to have him there to witness the occasion—she owed him so much.

Tim had been a volunteer at the orphanage, working with several children over the years throughout her childhood, and he had taken quite a shine to her. When he had learned of the position opening at his work, he had done everything humanly possible to help her get the 9-1-1 operator's job.

"I wondered if I had done something to offend you, Tim. I missed our daily conversations today," Cassie said. Happier than she'd ever been, she laughed at herself now—she'd been unhappy all night, knowing that Thad would not be there when she got home and thinking that Tim was avoiding her. It had been a big part of why this particular night had been so much more trying on her than most other nights. But now, all was forgiven and forgotten.

Since neither Thad nor Cassie had true family, they chose to continue with their daily focus, planning for a marriage—not a wedding. They quickly decided not to have a long, drawn-out engagement. The decision was mutual; three weeks later, the two would exchange vows and rings, and Cassie would take his last name. She realized that it would be the first time she had really had a last name.

Sure, she had been given a name at birth, but *Johnson* was little more than a term used to differentiate her from any other Cassies who came to live in the orphanage—which had happened only once in her eighteen years there, and the other Cassie had only stayed there for a few short months. But taking Thad's last name now gave her a sense of belonging, not something she had been acquainted with much in her younger days.

Thad and Cassie both made enough money to pay bills, but not much extra cash. There wasn't much leftover for extravagances. They both agreed that a modest destination wedding would be adequate. After all, their guest list would not consist of many people, since they both had lived somewhat reclusive lives with no family to speak of on either side. They invited Tammy and her husband, Steve, to accompany them on their special wedding weekend.

"Oh dear, thank you so much for thinking of us. We would love to join you on your special day," Tammy replied.

"But we will only accept your invitation if you allow us to pay all expenses," Steve continued.

Tammy and Steve had never had any children, and this seemed to fill a void for them, while at the same time helping the young couple.

"You know that we think of you as our daughter, don't you, Cassie?" Steve asked.

"We already decided months ago to pay for your wedding—whenever that day would arise. It's just something that we want to do for you both," Tammy stated, as though she were completing Steve's thought.

Cassie admired the way her landlords had adored one another and realized that was what she wanted in her marriage too. Steve and Tammy knew each other so well after all these years. They literally completed one another's thoughts—and sentences.

But for now, Cassie had to keep her mind focused on the present. It was time to figure out the details for their wedding. Both Cassie and Thad had spoken often of one place they wanted to visit together. While Thad's job had allowed him to see much of the country, neither of them had ever made their way to Memphis. Since it seemed to be the logical choice, and with the soon-to-be-wed couple's appreciative consent, Tammy asked if she could make the necessary arrangements. This was appealing to Thad and Cassie as it added a sense of mystery to the occasion. The young lovers knew they were heading to their desired destination but little else.

As Tammy and Steve turned to head back to their home, Thad put his arm around her waist and whispered, "I promise to love you forever."

"I don't know where my life would be without you, Thad, and I never want to find out," replied an enamored Cassie. "I too promise to love you forever, babe!" She found a comfortable nook to rest her tired head on his shoulder.

The loving neighbors had decided to make the wedding weekend much more than adequate— they wanted to make it magical for Thad and Cassie. While they didn't know Thad all that well yet, they had learned a bit about him, as the foursome had spent quite a few nights playing cards, dining in, or going out together on their nights off work.

It was 10:00 a.m. on a Friday morning in late April when the first wonderful surprise began. A knock at the door set the stage for the events to come. Cassie was beaming with joy as she opened the front door. But nothing could prepare her for the excitement she felt seeing the sharply dressed chauffer waiting to escort her to the white stretch limousine parked on the street. It was in the very same spot where, just weeks before, Thad had parked when he delivered that all-important question to her. As the chauffeur opened the limo door, she spotted Thad, sitting in the seat already, gleaming with pride. When she looked into his eyes, she knew beyond all else that she was truly loved.

"Was this your idea, Thad?" Cassie asked.

"No, ma'am. I thought we were all going to pile into my jeep...even got the tires rotated and oil changed for the occasion," he replied.

"It must have been our wonderful landlords. I hope they didn't go to a lot of trouble—" She was cut off by the doors opening to the limousine.

Tammy and Steve joined the happy couple in the luxurious vehicle. Thad was the first to comment on the uniqueness of this car. "It has the body style and power of a Dodge Charger but several attributes of a Lamborghini. This is possibly the most unique vehicle I have ever seen."

"It even has a hemi," Steve replied.

But one glance from Tammy told Steve that it was not a good time for manly car talk, so the conversation moved on quickly.

During the six-hour ride, along with her intended and the best neighbors she could have ever asked for,

Cassie sipped champagne and discussed the weekend to come. Much of the plans were still left undisclosed, especially to Cassie. As she glanced around the inside of the car, she spotted a large garment bag hanging and realized someone had even gone to the trouble of picking out a wedding gown for her.

"Tammy, my guess is that you were the one responsible for this. I had planned to wear a modest, ankle-length white dress," Cassie said.

Tammy winked at the young man who was about to make Cassie's life complete, and Cassie realized she was outnumbered here. She had never lived a fancy life and saw no reason why her wedding should stray too far from her ideals. This clearly was not a general consensus, however. It didn't take long for Cassie to realize that she was in for a weekend unlike anything she could have ever imagined. The idea suddenly didn't sound so bad to her, either. She decided to just go with the flow.

Time passed quickly as they concluded their journey down the interstate to the wedding destination. Thad and Cassie had both grown up with a beer lifestyle, but she quickly realized that they were about to share a champagne weekend. It had started from the moment she had opened her front door, but it was coming into full swing as the limo pulled up to the grand Peabody Hotel.

Cassie found herself completely pampered and catered to from the start. The doorman assisted as the limousine driver unloaded the bags from the back of his car, and the concierge summoned the bellhop to steer the luggage cart into the elevator and up to their rooms on the twelfth floor.

Cassie gazed in awe at the magnitude of this exquisite structure.

"This is perhaps the most luxurious hotel I have ever seen," Cassie said. "It must have cost you guys a fortune..."

But Tammy cut her short. "Please don't give money another thought. I want you kids to have a weekend that you will remember for the rest of your lives. For the next three days, money is not your concern!"

Shops lined the elegantly decorated lobby, which housed a bar near a fountain of swimming ducks. Still unsure of the actual details of the weekend, Cassie quickly learned to just listen to instructions by her co-travelers, playing along with their requests. She drank the last swallow of a fantastic margarita, seated in the comfortable area near the bar. She was then informed of an appointment on the lower level of the hotel.

"I have booked us a little spa time," said a very re-laxed Tammy. Cassie was a bit relieved to hear this, not as much for her own sake as for Tammy's. For the first time, she realized that Tammy possibly had needed a vacation more than the rest of the group. She had begun to look tired. Cassie had never noticed before, but Tammy was beginning to show her age.

Cassie followed Tammy through the halls and down the stairs to the basement of the Peabody Hotel, where she was escorted to an awaiting hot tub. After relaxing for an hour, allowing the rippling water to caress her skin, she was taken into an adjoining room for her next surprise: a deluxe pedicure. The truth was, any pedicure would have seemed deluxe to her, since she had never had one before.

"One final stop and we can kill a little time before we head back up to meet the guys," Tammy said as she stopped to schedule appointments with the hotel hairdresser.

Though she would have been content with a courthouse ceremony, followed by a barbecue in her backyard, all this fuss was actually making Cassie very happy. She was surprised to find how much the activities of the weekend pleased her, but she knew this was not a lifestyle she would ever feel comfortable with on a daily basis. However, for now, she was going to enjoy every minute of the plans Tammy had set.

"I never knew what *giddy* actually felt like before this weekend. I can't believe you went to so much trouble," Cassie said.

"I wanted to show you how much you, and now Thad too, mean to us. We couldn't love you more if you were our own children, and we are just tickled that you chose to include us in your special day," she replied.

Thad and Cassie had never really found time to make new friends, and they really hadn't needed to since her landlords had been so good for them both.

Meanwhile, the men had been working diligently to put the final touches on the weekend. Everything had been arranged, right down the tickets for a private trolley ride down the main streets of Memphis on Saturday afternoon.

Once the pampering had concluded, the group freshened up and prepared for an evening of merriment down on Beale Street. It was unseasonably warm for this time of year, and they all welcomed the opportunity to take in the sights, up close and personal, as they walked the short distance to where the nightlife began.

After a wonderful dinner at a fine-dining establishment along their path, they found themselves in an exciting Coyote Ugly. Since this weekend had already traveled far outside the norm for her, Cassie decided to leave her inhibitions packed away in her suitcase and live it up. At one point, she actually danced on the bar along with two of the waitresses. While she wouldn't have won any contests based on dance style, if spreading joy would have been a category for the judges, she would have certainly been a contender. She quickly noticed that, while the crowd was sparse, they seemed to be rather appreciative of her performance.

"Hey, sweetie, you can bring that performance over here," Thad heard one man say from his seat across the room. Shaking his head and laughing, he caught Cassie's hand and invited her down. While he'd enjoyed the show, he was hoping to see more of the Cassie he'd fallen in love with.

She'd never seen him get jealous—but then, she'd really given him reason. Cassie climbed down, and the group decided to consider another bar to conclude their last evening of bachelor- and bachelorette-hood.

With what seemed to be an unlimited supply of drinks before her on the bar, a slightly intoxicated Cassie agreed—and then expressed her wish to see what other sights existed in this unfamiliar town.

After a short walk down the sidewalk, she spotted a white Cadillac resting under the pavilion of yet another bar that was owned by one of her favorite musicians. After a brief discussion, they decided to make this their next stop, and they found an Elvis impersonator to be the entertainment of the evening.

One final drink at the bar made them realize they needed to retreat back to their rooms for the remainder of the evening. By this time, street performers had come out in full force. They performed and a jazz band played songs as the group made their way back to the hotel.

"I just can't get over this room, honey. It's unlike anything I have ever seen before—or expect that I will see ever again," Cassie informed Thad as he closed the hotel room door behind them. Cassie was still amazed at the splendor everywhere she turned.

Moments later, Cassie heard a chuckle coming from the bathroom; Thad had realized that the soaps were yellow and shaped like rubber duckies. He pointed out an actual rubber ducky lying on the sink as well. At this point, Cassie realized that her truck driver felt displaced, as he said, "I feel a bit high society here, babe. I had to unwrap decorative tissue paper and ribbon from the toilet paper."

The couple shared one last bottle of champagne, which had been placed in the room for them. And then a knock at the door revealed an unexpected nighttime appetizer, ordered by Tammy and Steve. Before they knew it, the clock had advanced, and it was technically their wedding day.

"I seriously need sleep," Cassie declared, and Thad overwhelmingly agreed.

Neither of them was given to superstition, so they felt little reluctance to staying in the room together on their final night as single individuals. Cassie wanted nothing more than to awaken in his arms on her wedding day, and he returned those same feelings. They both knew right where they wanted to be—and that's exactly where they were.

They closed their eyes, and both realized that this would undoubtedly be a trip to remember.

W hile Tammy wished she had thought this one up herself, the next event was completely on Thad.

In the morning, Thad snuck out of his and Cassie's room, releasing his arms quietly from around the woman he so deeply loved. At this point, Tammy and Steve had opened their door to allow him entry. No sooner had he shut the door than four sharply dressed gentlemen carrying a selection of string instruments planted themselves directly outside Cassie and Thad's hotel-room door. Starting softly, so as not to startle her or other guests within earshot, they began playing a series of love songs. Thad had spent many hours on the road listening to a wide array of songs of varying genres, so it wasn't too difficult for his heart to select the most romantic songs, expressing how much he loved her.

Thad knew Cassie wished to wake up in his arms, and he returned those feelings. But he also knew that it would be much more difficult for them to part once they both were awake and he knew that they both had a lot to get done on this special day. So he followed his head rather than his heart.

Cassie's eyes slowly opened as she first heard the sweet sounds of *I Will Always Love You* playing outside her door. "Thad, where is that music coming from?" she asked. She realized that he was no longer there, and a brief sadness filled her heart.

But then Cassie fully awakened to remember that she was in the beautiful hotel room in Memphis on her wedding day!

"Thad?" she called again, thinking he was in the bathroom, but she soon noticed that the dress clothes he had packed for the day were no longer in their room.

She heard a knock at their door. "Thad, where have you been?" Cassie asked, concerned, as she opened the door. But it wasn't Thad standing on the other side.

Tammy stood alone in the hallway with the most beautiful bouquet of flowers in her outreached arms. "Here is your bridal bouquet. Now come on, sweetie. We have a busy day ahead of us."

Once Cassie had composed herself, the girls headed down to the lobby for a wonderful breakfast in the hotel restaurant. After Cassie swallowed the final sip of coffee from her cup, the two women proceeded out the door, toward the lobby. They took a brief detour and spent a couple of minutes browsing the shops that lined the lobby before finding a seat close to the elevators.

Tammy had researched this morning's event, and she did not intend to miss it. As the elevators slid open, a man dressed in uniform and carrying what appeared to be a wand led...a line of ducks. They marched down the carpet laid just for them, up the small set of stairs, and into the fountain where they would spend the day. It was a magnificent sight, one Cassie was happy to witness, but she couldn't get Thad off her mind.

At one point, she thought she caught sight of him amid the crowd standing along the rail on the upper floor of the lobby. However, when she glanced back, he was nowhere to be found. It was approaching time for lunch, and Cassie still had no idea of the plans for the day. She was beginning to feel a bit of anxiety.

A trip back to the hot tub, followed by an appointment to get their hair done, would finish up the morning for Cassie, with the closest person she had ever known to a mother.

They returned to Cassie's room to prepare for the ceremony. As they walked inside, they spotted the freshly placed room service cart in the corner: a delicious meal left for them. Once they finished, Cassie opened the bag containing her wedding dress. It was the first time she had laid eyes upon it. She was a rather simple girl, and she had been concerned that the dress would be too much.

As she unzipped the garment bag, Cassie gasped. "Oh, Tammy! This is the most beautiful dress I have ever seen. You really shouldn't have."

The simple street-length dress, made almost exclusively of white satin, was pretty but not overly elegant. Only a few strategically placed sequins adorned the tasteful lace-covered bodice, giving it just enough flair to make her look like the princess Thad believed her to be.

"I tried very hard to stay within the boundaries of beautifully elegant but not extravagant. I think you will look like an angel in this dress, Cassie," Tammy replied.

There was also a second dress tucked behind the gown. Tammy quickly changed into the simple dress, appropriate for an informal wedding.

Once Cassie had put her dress on and Tammy had added a few of the flowers from the bouquet into Cassie's flowing hair, the two women decided that it was time to continue on with the events of the day.

"You are such a beautiful bride, Cassie. It means the world to Steve and I that you and Thad have included us in this occasion, you know," Tammy said tearfully.

"You and Steve have become the parents I never had over the past several years. I really can't imagine not sharing this day with you two. Thank you for everything you have done," Cassie replied through her own stream of tears. It was fortunate that Cassie didn't believe in wearing makeup as she surely would have been sporting black streaks on her beautifully glowing cheeks before the day came to a close.

Thad and Cassie had been adamant of one thing during the planning stage of this wedding: that they would be writing their own vows. While Thad was a man of few words, he wanted the words they were basing their life together upon to be theirs, not anyone else's. Cassie didn't even write hers down. She was so sure of the feelings in her heart that she knew it would not be a problem to let the words just flow.

It had now been several hours since she had laid eyes upon her soul mate, even if it had been him standing up against the railing during the duck march. She missed him so very much. It was an emotion that she generally dismissed. After all, he spent more time gone during the work week than he did near her. But this was different. She knew he was close, and it was killing her not to be with him. It was abundantly clear to her that she was ready to become his wife.

With Tammy leading the way, Cassie realized that her dreams were about to come true. The time had come for her to say "I do." But she still had little idea of what lay ahead for the day. They stood on the corner of the street in front of the hotel, awaiting what Cassie assumed was would be a car. She soon found that she was wrong, when she spotted the trolley coming over the crest of the hill.

The red trolley car was adorned with flowing ribbons and bows. As it drew closer, she noticed something else familiar—attached to the outside of the trolley car was the banner that read WILL YOU MARRY ME, CASSIE? that had graced Thad's trailer just three weeks prior.

Her face shone with the brightest smile ever seen as she saw Thad standing in the back of the trolley car. Tammy wondered if they should be watching for landing planes—they might mistake the glow about Cassie for runway lights.

Cassie stepped up into the trolley, expecting to find it crowded with tourists. Instead, it contained just four individuals: the driver, a clergyman, and the two most important men in her life, awaiting her arrival. If she had looked up at the digital marquee on the front of the trolley, she would have seen that it read CONGRATULATIONS, MR. & MRS. MALONE.

"Wow, it's just us on here?" Cassie asked astonishingly.

"Yes, my love, it is all for you," Thad replied.

"Well, actually it is for both of you, Thad," Steve corrected.

As the trolley began slowly descending the hill, the clergyman proceeded with the ceremony. Up until now, Cassie had half believed herself in a dream. "Thad Malone, do you take this woman to be your lawfully wedded wife?"

"I do," were the only words he had to say, and they were more than enough for her to hear.

"And do you, Cassandra Marie Johnson, take this man to be your lawfully wedded husband, to have and to hold from this day forward?" the reverend continued.

He had barely finished his words before she bolted out, "I do too."

It was then time for the vows they had chosen for themselves. "Cassie, you have brought so much joy into my life. Before you, I merely *existed* in a world where I now *live*! I intend to spend the rest of my days making you smile. Please don't ever question my love for you—you are my life, and I love you with all my heart," Thad said.

Cassie felt dampness hitting her blushing cheeks once more, but she spotted a slight tear in his eyes as well. It was clear that Thad too was feeling overcome with emotion. He had been alone for so many years before she had come into his life just over a year ago, and he really hadn't dreamed that life would ever be any other way for him. But something else dawned upon Cassie: he had said all of those words without a single stutter. He had truly meant every single word he had just said. It was as if his heart were speaking directly to hers for the very first time ever.

It was Cassie's turn, and she felt almost intimidated by the words he'd spoken. But she realized that it wasn't a competition, and she redirected. "Thad, you have made me feel whole. You have been my knight in shining armor, beginning with the moment you parked your semi behind my car. From the moment we met, I discovered safety in your arms." She continued on for a while longer. Cassie had so much to say. But she knew that she had a lifetime to show him just how much he meant to her—always! She concluded by proclaiming her unending love for him.

Thad, overcome with the feelings of the moment, didn't wait for permission to kiss his wife. As though he had been practicing, he swept her up into his arms and reminded her that she was his, and that was the way it would always be. Cassie cried steadily as she wrapped her arms around his neck and returned the kiss with more passion than she had ever thought herself capable of, while the cool breeze flowed in from the open windows surrounding them.

At the conclusion of the ceremony, the minister announced them to the few attendees as Mr. and Mrs. Thad Malone, and it suddenly felt so real. For the first time in her entire life, Cassie knew where she belonged.

The weekend of merriment and celebration drew to an end, and the couple returned to their daily lives. How could it be that so much had changed, yet so much remained the same?

Thad had been spending much of the time he'd had off the road at her house; he was practically living there already anyway. Cassie had known that he would give her space anytime she really needed it. She'd just never really needed it. She enjoyed the time they shared and always longed for his safe return whenever he made his leave.

It only seemed natural that they would make her place their home, and it didn't require much to add his belongings to her already homey household. Since he had spent so little time in any one place up until now, he really didn't own much stuff. Little more than a suitcase was necessary to transport his possessions.

The summer was filled with weekends of barbecues and card games with Tammy and Steve. They continued on in much the same manner and returned to their daily routines, hardly missing a beat along the way. On the surface, the changes in their lives were hardly noticeable. But there was one major change that stood out to those close to Cassie—she had found a place she could call home, in her heart. While the four walls remained the same, the house she had resided in for several years now was much more than just a house. It was now a home.

Thad made it his lot in life to show her the world as he had learned to see it. On any typical Sunday morning, they would jump into the car and drive in a random direction until he felt the urge to stop. The day would proceed consistently from there in one respect: Cassie had learned to remain seated, patiently awaiting her knight in shining armor to open the passenger door. With arm outreached, he'd pull her into his arms and say, "Walk with me, my love," or something similar. Cassie wanted nothing more than to oblige. So with her hand in his, they would meander about whatever surroundings were nearby.

On one particular excursion, they had been driving along a scenic river road when Cassie spotted a fawn lying calmly along a nearby bike path. Fearing that it had been injured, Thad pulled onto the shoulder and watched the baby for several minutes as she lay there. He was an avid hunter, but he also had compassion for the animals that he hunted. It was difficult for Thad and Cassie both to witness a hurt animal, so he grabbed his cell phone and called the local authorities. The minutes turned into hours as they awaited their arrival, but no one came.

During the three hours they sat there, the defenseless little deer still didn't move.

The couple spent the time just talking. "Did you notice how tired Tammy has been? I noticed it while we were in Memphis, and I just thought it was the excitement of the weekend. I know that she put a lot of time into planning that trip, but she doesn't seem to be feeling much better" Cassie said.

"Yeah, I did notice. Steve and I were talking about that the other day out in the yard. He is trying to talk her into going to the doctor, but she's resisting," Thad replied.

Cassie frowned. "Maybe I should talk with her about it."

Just then, the conversation was interrupted as a state trooper pulled alongside the bike path and approached

Thad's window. "You called in about an injured deer?" questioned the officer.

"Yes, she is lying still over on the bike path. We got out of the car and walked over to get a closer look, but she never even attempted to move. It looks as though she is suffering with a broken leg," replied Thad.

The police officer walked back and popped his trunk, reached in, and retrieved a rifle. As the baby heard the cocking of the gun, she suddenly bolted into the outer edge of the woods. The obviously uninjured deer stopped and stared back at the two men, who now just stood in amazement. That little one had allowed Cassie and Thad to walk within feet of it without the least hint of anxiety. It was not until she heard the warning sign of immediate danger that fear even had begun to play a part. It was as if the deer could sense that Cassie and Thad loved nature and the wonders of it all.

O nce they arrived back home, Thad shared the story with their landlords while the group gathered around the barbecue grill in the backyard.

Meanwhile, Cassie and Tammy sat at the table, sipping tea. Cassie brought up her concerns about Tammy's health.

Reluctantly, Tammy agreed to make an appointment since she too had realized that something was wrong.

Cassie and Steve sat by her side as she anxiously awaited the results when the doctor called her in for a consultation three days later.

While the news hit Tammy so hard, no one noticed the effect it was having on Steve as well. He turned his life's focus on to her and rarely left her side.

During the next several months together, Tammy found it difficult to leave the house so Cassie and Thad shared many wonderful memories with them at home.

Eight months later, Tammy succumbed to her battle with cancer and they shared great sadness when Cassie, Thad and Steve had to say an eternal good-bye to Tammy. Cassie tried to find comfort in the thought that her friend had not spent years in agony.

Even though her suffering ended quickly, this battle took its toll on them all —-but nothing like it had done to Steve. He'd watched this horrible disease rapidly take away the spirit that had flowed so freely within the woman he had loved with all of his heart.

Cassie took a brief leave of absence from her job in order to help Steve battle a severe bout of depression, as he tried to come to terms with the emptiness Tammy's death had left him with. However, Cassie felt like a failure when, after six months of living with a broken heart, Steve gave up the fight and took his own life.

While he didn't want to rush her back to work, Thad realized that he had to keep Cassie moving forward in this life, now that she had lost the only people who had loved her like parents would. She missed them terribly. After months of subtle encouragement from Thad, she returned to work. Cassie threw herself into her job and it seemed to be her primary driving force.

Cassie worked overtime at making sure that others didn't have to suffer grief the way she had felt it during Tammy's and Steve's deaths. Whenever a 9-1-1 call came in, she would resolve it with more diligence than all of her coworkers combined.

But there was still so much sadness in Cassie's eyes. Thad felt helpless to comfort her, and even more so every time he would pull his big rig onto the highway that led him away from her. He knew that, every time he left, she felt even more lost. But he had little choice. He had bills to pay, and he hoped that she realized that too.

More than ever now, Thad wondered if they should try to have children—not so much for his sake, but primarily for hers. They had both agreed, however, early in their relationship that their careers were far too demanding to allow for children—and besides, they were both inexperienced with how to handle children. They had decided not to even consider the thought. Now Cassie and Thad were relatively alone most of the time, and he often wondered if Cassie felt that their relationship was still enough.

He pulled her in close every chance he could. But he also realized that the road would be pulling him away more than toward her. Much like she had suffered while witnessing Steve dealing with depression, Thad now watched as Cassie's smile became less and less frequent—until one day he just could no longer bear the sight.

At first he considered taking on extra-long hauls, but soon realized that she needed him there, and while their vows hadn't stated such, he had promised in his heart to love her for better or worse—and this was definitely the "worse" part.

He realized that he couldn't allow her to follow the path they had watched Steve travel. So one day, for what seemed like no reason in particular, he once again scooped Cassie into his arms and promised to love her forever. He reminded her that loss is part of life and that she was going to have to find a way to fight through it. So together as often as they could be for weeks, they found a way to battle her demons.

He found that the more firmly he held her, the easier it became for Cassie to smile. After several months of Thad expressing his undying love toward her, Cassie found a way to not only smile again, but to return almost completely to the woman she had been when they met. In many ways, he actually recognized that she had possibly even grown from the experience.

Cassie's coworkers marveled at the strength of their love. They too had watched as their friend had struggled and were ever so pleased when she returned to the happy, carefree girl they had once known.

Thad and Cassie resumed their weekend road trips, and the rough edges that had existed between them during the previous couple of years seemed to smooth out in time. Life had once more become the existence she had longed for—with her one true love by her side.

he happy couple spent the next fifteen years wrapped up in each other's lives—and arms! But if life had taught Cassie anything, it was this: life is full of twists and turns, and it's never a good idea to become so secure that you assume tomorrow will simply be a repeat of yesterday. Life is about change.

Then one day, Cassie found out just how cruel fate can be. The day had played itself out much like any other, and it was time for her to head out to the police station. She grabbed a light jacket from the hook next to the front door and shouted her normal, "I'm heading to work. I will see you tomorrow. Have a safe journey tonight. Love ya, babe."

Thad called back with his typical response, which wafted up the stairs from their bedroom below: "Good night, sweetheart. I love you too. See you in the morning."

So far, there was nothing unusual about that night, and there was no reason to believe there should be. She closed the front door behind her and continued on in her typical happy-go-lucky demeanor to her office downtown.

Cassie liked the idea of answering 9-1-1 calls during the time Thad was working. It almost made her feel close to him in a strange way. Living in the heart of St. Louis, he also appreciated the fact that she was not sitting home by herself while he was out driving.

Meanwhile, Thad prepared for his night of work. He enjoyed driving his semi, especially during the night-time hours when the roads were nearly vacant. He had been a truck driver for years before he had met Cassie.

At times, she wondered how a man who had been so obviously content with bachelorhood could so easily conform to married life, but somehow it seemed easy for Thad.

Every day, Thad told Cassie, "I promise to love you forever," and she believed every word. Thad had not been a man who spoke for just any reason, and she quickly learned to cherish whatever he had to say.

They said their customary good-nights just moments before she left for work. Cassie left as Thad was preparing to pack his lunch, and then he too was off to work for the night. She looked forward him greeting her when she arrived home from work the next morning. He had a short haul slated for this particular night. Just a quick trip up to the state capitol and back, and then he would be home for several days. These days of closeness thrilled her.

But life dealt Cassie an unfair hand on this particular day.

"Hello, you've reached the 9-1-1 operator. What is the nature of your emergency?" Cassie asked.

A winded caller on the line replied, "I just came upon a tractor-trailer accident out on the interstate."

At first, Cassie continued the call with her calm demeanor, as she knew it was part of her job to ease the minds of those calling. She had dealt with so many trucking-accident calls during her years that, while her heart would skip a beat each time, she was able to remain composed and continue helping the callers. But this time something was different. As the details unfolded, her heart sank. The caller had discovered the wreckage, overturned and almost completely engulfed in flames, next to the roadside. The only identifying mark he spotted on the vehicle was a giant red rose painted on what remained of the trailer. But it too had been destroyed by the time the caller had connected with Cassie.

The next thing Cassie knew her coworkers were standing over her—she was lying flat on the floor next to her desk. One of her coworkers had picked up her headset from the floor and completed the call. Soon the paramedics arrived and began getting her rapid heartbeat back to at least close to normal.

They then confirmed what she feared: Thad had in fact perished.

$\mathcal{L}$ife suddenly became more difficult than she could have ever imagined. What she had relied upon as destiny suddenly took a sharp turn as life drew its ugly fangs and took away her most important constant. In the blink of an eye, her whole life changed during the worst night of her life. Eventually, Cassie would remember that it had some good. But for a time, all she could see was the bad.

Several neighbors were waiting at her house when Tim brought Cassie home from work that night, once the EMTs had given her the green light to leave. If she had had her wits about her, she would have asked how the neighbors had already learned the news. But she was so confused and lost that Cassie didn't even notice anyone was there. Quite a crowd had gathered; they all had grown quite fond of both Cassie and Thad over the years. He had always been willing to pitch in with any of their projects whenever he had had the time.

At the end of what had turned into a very long day, Cassie tried to sleep but wondered if she would ever sleep again. She questioned whether there was any point in sleeping or eating. She was having difficulty determining whether there was any point to anything anymore. Though she could barely comprehend her surroundings for those first several days, she was never alone—but she felt so alone.

Roger, a young college professor, had bought and moved into Tammy and Steve's house a few years prior. He soon became her rock as he stayed by her side for weeks. He escorted her to the funeral home and held her hand while she made the necessary arrangements. There were no visitation or graveside services held, just a simple memorial service for the grieving widow, coworkers, and a few close friends—neighbors mostly.

As Roger's car backed out of the parking spot at the funeral home, Cassie heard something familiar but painful playing on the radio. Their song had once made her smile. But now all comfort was gone for her. She thought about the very first time Thad had requested it, in that bar in Memphis, as they danced for the first time as husband and wife. Cassie wondered if she could ever listen to music again. How could she cope?

Weeks later, as Cassie emerged from the haze she had resided in since the moment she'd heard of Thad's death, she realized that time had not stopped, though her life seemed to be standing still.

Thad's remains now rested in a bronze urn upon the fireplace, which had been the backdrop for many romantic events during their years together. Next to the urn lay a completely silent clock that had been a special wedding present for the couple, given to them by the two people who had made that weekend in Memphis so special, before they had passed on from this world. Cassie glanced at the clock and realized that it had fallen silent. She no longer cared. It could just remain silent—she felt no need for time any longer. The only thing on her mind was that Thad was gone, and she had never even gotten the chance to say good-bye.

After her extensive leave of absence, Cassie felt it impossible to ever return to the office, much less to the phone. It was with much sadness that she tendered her resignation, and even more disappointment shone on the face of her boss as he accepted the paperwork. Cassie wasn't sure how she was going to make ends meet now, but again, she didn't seem to care. All she could see was a long, dark tunnel instead of a life, and she wondered how she would ever return to life, much less be happy again.

It seemed to Cassie as though, everywhere she went, people greeted her with a head tilt and unending sympathy. But she didn't want sympathy—she wanted Thad. His existence was the only thing that had made her life fulfilling, and she would never be able to accept anything less. Now, with no job and no husband, she had no idea where to turn or what to do next. She began cleaning out closets, drawers, anything she could find just to keep busy.

Simple days now seemed long gone, and Cassie found herself almost daily implementing Thad's rule for strength and guidance, especially now that he was no longer in her world to help. Her saving grace would be to keep too busy to think about life, to not let depression dig a hole too deep for her to climb out of, alone!

But all Cassie could think about was that forever with Thad had not lasted nearly long enough, and these were thoughts that she would have to put aside if she was ever to find happiness again.

A dream one night gave Cassie some much-needed willpower. Thad appeared, standing by her bedside. He nestled up to her and pulled her close. The couple lay next to one another, and at first there was complete silence. They simply eased each other's pain, holding one another close. After a while, Thad apologized for leaving her. He used that soft-spoken tone so distinctive of him. For a moment, she believed he was in the room.

"I never meant to leave you, and I hope that you understand I had no choice. Please know that my love for you has not died. Now I have to ask you to do what you will perceive as impossible at first, but it must be done. You must build yourself a new life—without me!"

When Cassie awoke several hours later, she discovered her arms wrapped around her own body, as though she had been hugging herself. For the first time in months, the widow felt a sense of peace. Now consciously awake, she felt overwhelmed with the feeling that he had been right next to her. She even questioned whether she smelled a hint of his cologne. But that sense had come before, and though she knew that he had not physically been there, a strong feeling of warmth came over her, and she knew that the words that she'd dreamed him saying were right. It was time to begin a new life—without him.

That marked the beginning of a rebirth for her. She packed a few bags and decided to start exploring the world that Thad had always promised to show her, that he would have succeeded to show her, had he still been by her side.

In a way, she would always mourn the loss of the years she had been left to live alone following Thad's accident.

She stopped by the bank and pulled out some of the money that Tammy and Steve had left her all those years ago. Cassie had been in so much pain back when she lost them that she had vowed never to touch that money. But now she knew what gut-wrenching pain really was, and she just wanted to escape, in any way possible.

Her first stop was St. Louis, Missouri, at the orphanage that had been the only childhood home she had ever known. She was surprised to find that the historical structure still stood tall, though it didn't house nearly as many children as it had when she'd lived there. Cassie was pleased when the administrator took time out of her busy schedule to give her a tour of the building.

"It seems so much smaller than I recall," Cassie said.

"It's because you were so much smaller back then," the administrator said, smiling. "I hear that a lot from the former orphans who return for visits."

The tour came to a close and Cassie had to decide where to go next. The only real decision that she had made prior to leaving her home that morning was that she had no intention of returning for a while.

As she had always had a fondness for animals of all kinds, her next stop was the nearby zoo. It had been a childhood dream of hers to spend days just gazing into the cages that were home to so many animals.

Cassie realized that, in order to build this new life, she had to revisit her childhood dreams and desires and then explore new paths derived from who she had been as a child. When she got to the front gate, the first thing she laid eyes upon was the elephant statue, which seemed to be welcoming her back not just to the zoo, but to the world.

Cassie envisioned Thad acting as though he was getting ready to go on some wild jungle hunt. She recalled their previous visits here as she proceeded through the gates and down the paved pathway.

Cassie concluded her day by pulling her car into a long-term parking spot at the airport. She had never flown anywhere and decided that it was about time to find out what it was like. She walked into the airport and up to the closest airline counter. "Where is your next flight heading?" Cassie asked.

The woman behind the counter replied, "The next available flight would be Charlotte, North Carolina. Would you like to purchase a ticket?"

Cassie replied with a hesitant yes. With that, she picked up her packed bags and proceeded in the direction the woman advised, toward the security checkpoint. Cassie found the airport security procedures a little tedious, but what did she know? It's not like she had any past experience to reference.

Having been married to a man who seemed almost bound to the road, Cassie had never found occasion to board one of the silver eagles she had watched fly overhead, from her window at the orphanage.

She found it a little nerve wracking as security searched through her intimate items. With that experience now behind her, Cassie sat at the gate awaiting the announcement to board the big silver bird. Time seemed to slow as she stared out the glass wall, watching the vessel as it pulled into the allotted space in the vast area outdoors.

She watched with wonder as the pilot parked the plane with such precision that it was as if he were guiding a small compact car into a space in the grocery-store parking lot. But this was certainly no grocery store, and he was definitely not steering a compact car. She recalled a conversation that she had had once, when she was a small child, with one of the older orphans about his parents taking him to the airport to stand at the gate and watch planes take off and land for hours. With that discussion in mind, Cassie realized how much things had changed following recent events in the United States. No one would be allowed to just watch planes from the window she was gazing through now—too much security to ever allow that. Cassie wouldn't have been allowed entry to that part of the airport without a boarding pass.

The solid door opened, and an enormous mass of people, dragging behind them a wide assortment of rolling bags, came marching from within. Soon the last arriving passengers left the gate area in search of the baggage carousel, and the flight attendant announced that boarding would now commence. With her boarding pass clasped in one hand and the scant amount of luggage she had packed for her undetermined destination gripped in the other, Cassie awaited permission to approach the walkway.

She was seated next to a man so stout that he pressed her against the outer wall of the plane. He must have read the fear on her face; he moved to a less-occupied row of seats just prior to takeoff. Cassie was thankful to have the space to herself, though she had had a lot of that during the months leading to this trip. She just wanted to soak up as much of the experience as she could, not feel the need to entertain a stranger in conversation.

She caught herself gasping as the plane made its initial ascent. "Would you like a drink?" asked the petite girl pushing a beverage cart down the aisle.

Cassie thought for a moment. "Do you have champagne?" It was at that moment that the lonely woman decided to remove herself from the box where her grief had placed her. It was time to experience the finer side of life, like she had discovered during her wedding weekend all those years ago—when she had been surrounded by so much love.

Three hours later, the plane touched down, and it was time for Cassie to consider the next phase of her journey. For tonight, she would just stay at a nearby hotel, provided she could find one.

She decided to leave the hotel destination up to the taxi driver. Cassie began to learn how to just let life live itself. She had no other intention than to just exist for a while—and she was actually learning how to do it well—possibly for the first time in her life.

She booked the executive suite at the finest hotel the cab driver could recommend. The view from her window was breathtaking. Even though she had grown up in a big city, one with many tall buildings, these seemed to glisten in the sunlight as she opened her rested eyes the next morning. A good night's sleep was a refreshing change for her as normal slumber had never fully returned after Thad's accident.

Since she had nowhere in particular to go, she decided to spend the day in her hotel room. As she looked out onto the street below, Cassie spotted a trolley that took her back to a special day. She thought back to that trip to Memphis twenty years ago and realized that she had so much to be thankful for in her life. She'd had something that most go a whole lifetime without—and she might have been greedy to assume she was entitled to that for an entire lifetime. This realization was definitely a turning point in her grief journey. Cassie revised her plan for the day, ventured down to the street below, bought a day pass to ride, and boarded that trolley. She just sat there, speaking to no one, and enjoyed the view for the better part of the day.

After several hours of shopping, sightseeing, and meandering about the city, she enjoyed a dinner at one of the finest restaurants the city had to offer. This too was a leap for her. Cassie had never been a fan of dining alone, and her meals had been reduced to whatever a drive-through could provide.

Cassie accomplished more in her two days in North Carolina than she could have ever deemed possible; therefore, she decided to return home to attempt to rebuild a life for herself there. With bags in tow, she once more hailed a cab and was on her way back to the airport. This time, since she knew her destination, Cassie just watched the people around her as she sat, waiting to board the next silver bird home.

As she boarded the plane and took her place in the only available window seat, she was pleased when a slightly older woman seated herself in the aisle seat next to her just before the plane began its taxi to the runway. As *The Lake House* began playing as the onboard entertainment, she decided that conversation would be a welcome distraction.

The two introduced themselves, and Cassie began discussing her life with Dawn, a pleasant conversationalist. The two women discussed everything from politics, to religion, to family. Cassie's newfound travel companion offered her condolences as Cassie spoke of her loss. And for the first time since the day Thad had vanished from her life, she felt the stranger's offerings unnecessary. She really had, deep in her heart, realized that her time with him had been a positive part of her life. She just smiled and politely said, "Thank you."

Dawn must have sensed the sincerity in her reply; she commended Cassie on her inspirational attitude. Cassie didn't see her attitude that way, though. She just knew that she was doing what she needed to, to make it through to tomorrow. She felt sadness as the flight began to descend. She had never been one to take in strangers, but now Cassie felt compelled to obtain contact information for her new friend. Dawn willingly obliged her request, and a new and strong bond was formed. Cassie discovered that they didn't live that far from each other, and they vowed to stay in touch.

As she drove through the gate of the parking garage, Cassie officially recognized her new appreciation for the life she had been given.

The drive home was uneventful, but her inspiration seemed to fade somewhat as she put the car in park and walked up to the front steps of the house she had called home for her entire adult life. Cassie realized that everything she had once found endearing about her little home in the country had now become unbearable, and she felt truly alone once more.

Just as she was placing her foot on the top step leading to the house, Roger came around from his home out back to welcome her. He was pleased to see a positive change in her. But at the same time, he also saw a forlorn look in her eyes as she arrived back at the home she had shared with Thad for so long.

Two days later, after jet lag had become an issue of the past, Cassie invited Roger over for a simple dinner of grilled hamburgers and potato salad. Once the table was cleared and the dishes washed, Cassie advised him of the purpose for the invitation. "You know that I value your opinion very much. While I have not completely thought this through, I am considering moving away from here. But this is not a decision I intend to make in haste. I just wanted you to be the first to know."

Cassie saw the sadness enter his eyes with every word she said, but at the same time, she was quite certain that he understood.

Roger hadn't known Thad for nearly as long as she had—and not nearly as well. But he had witnessed the painful days she had encountered since his passing. "I completely understand, Cassie. You have my support. I know this is not an easy decision for you. But know that I will indeed miss you," Roger replied.

So her search began. In theory, she knew this was a good idea, but the economy had other ideas. After a few months of looking for a suitable purchaser, Cassie received a blank manila colored envelope in the mail. It didn't contain a return address, and the contact information was simply a toll-free number with instructions to call with regards to an offer to purchase her home. Cassie was concerned but intrigued, so she called. Expecting to hear a business introduction on the other end of the line, she felt disappointment mix with a bit more intrigue as a woman's voice merely answered with a business-like *hello*. At the conclusion of the telephone conversation, the woman advised Cassie to watch for a contract to purchase being sent by messenger later that day.

As the clock approached 4:00 p.m., Cassie began to sense a hoax, since there had still been no knock at the door. It didn't matter; she had nowhere to go anyway. But then, moments later, a black sedan arrived and a sharply dressed man with topcoat and hat removed himself from the driver's seat and proceeded up the walkway.

Realizing the validity of the offer, Cassie began to tremble as she opened the envelope left by the driver. She felt validated when she noticed the sizable offer noted inside. Cassie began to read every inch of the contract before her, noticing that it was far too good to be true. But there was nothing, even in the small print, to give her any reason for alarm. In fact, the terms were extremely generous, and the only drawback was a rather short time frame to vacate. The monetary terms made up for that, even though she hadn't even begun to search for a new place to call home.

She thought about how she had acquired her home, as well as the one out back where her dear friends and landlords had once lived. They had been so much like parents to her as she had begun life as an adult. Tammy and Steve had made her almost forget what it had felt like to be the shy little orphan girl she had once been. Cassie had not ultimately achieved ownership of her house, or the small home on the adjacent lot via money; it had been left to her by Tammy and Steve in their will—a slight consolation for the deaths of her friends but a consolation nevertheless. For some reason, she had never really thought about it in those terms before. But now she wondered if they would have approved of her decision to sell.

Roger was still sad at the prospect of Cassie moving from the neighborhood, but he also realized that it was probably the best option for her. He vowed to visit her, even if she moved thousands of miles away. They had developed a bond much like that of a brother and sister. And while he had always been there to fulfill her emotional needs it didn't seem likely that he would ever be capable of fulfilling her physical desires.

But Roger had become a godsend for her as he'd helped her sort through her heart for just the right home. They both had realized that she was not restricted to remain anywhere in particular. For the first time in her life, the possibilities were basically without boundaries. She had no real ties, and she was beginning to feel eager about the prospect of exploring her options. Cassie considered moving to other parts of the country, and realized that she would welcome a refreshing view in her daily life.

Just days after she received the mysterious offer on the house, Cassie was pleased to see a familiar name appear on her caller ID. She thought back to just a few short months ago when that friendly stranger had sat down in the seat next to her on the plane, and the two had made an immediate connection. They had not spoken much since that day. Cassie had gotten busy with her efforts to make the house ready for sale. Now she had the house pretty much sold and was happy to reconnect with Dawn.

"I have been thinking a lot about you lately. How are you?" Dawn began.

"I have been thinking about you lately too. I'm fine, but I've been very busy," Cassie replied.

When Cassie informed her of the offer to purchase her home and her intent to find a new home, Dawn offered her assistance to help Cassie relocate to Smithton, the place that she, herself, had always called home.

"I have a few connections in the real-estate industry and would be more than happy to put out a few feelers for you if you like," Dawn continued. Cassie eagerly accepted and a close friendship began developing between the two ladies.

The search began online for Cassie, while Dawn made it her personal mission to help her new friend in any way possible. Dawn's search took her on a wide hunt, since she wasn't exactly sure what Cassie's tastes would lead to. The truth of the matter was that Cassie wasn't sure either. She had spent all of her life, up to this point, living by necessity. It was an unfamiliar concept for her to base her search on the idea of *want*. But together, they narrowed the search considerably in a rather short amount of time. Cassie's online search revealed a piece of property that seemed to call out to her in some way. While the purchase price was steep, she really liked what she saw—then and upon further inspection.

Dawn took a drive, after receiving the request from Cassie, to look over the property. It was for sale by owner, and Cassie wasn't having much success in actually speaking with the owners. But from the outside, the home appeared to be well kept.

Cassie soon realized just how eager her friend had been to help her, as she answered the phone early one morning.

"Good morning, Cassie. I know that you liked that house on Stone Hill, but I have found another home that I feel you might like. It is immaculate in appearance," Dawn rambled in excitement.

Cassie took down the phone number from Dawn during their conversation. Dawn had placed the call while standing in the yard, looking directly at the rather unprofessional FOR SALE sign in front. Dawn had tried to call the number listed first, but she had had no luck in actually getting in touch with anyone.

Cassie decided to check things out for herself, so she dialed the number to the house that had won Dawn's vote.

"Hello?" said the voice on the other end of the line.

"Good morning. My name is Cassie Malone, and I am calling about the house that you have for sale in Smithton."

"Ah, yes," the woman replied. "I am taking care of the property for the owners. They are rather anxious to sell that home. The owners were transferred out of the country, and in fact, the price has just been reduced."

Cassie was relieved to have found such a great deal, just hours away from the place she had grown to call home. Even though she was starting over, she liked that it was possible to visit her old world when she needed to—at least the parts of that life that still remained.

But there was one drawback. Because of the urgency of the deal, Cassie had been unable to personally explore the property. Dawn, living so close, had had the opportunity to somewhat check out the inside and had advised her of its appeal.

Two weeks later, she stopped by the title company with check in hand, purchasing this home for less than a quarter of its market value. The whole home-buying process went so quickly and Cassie had to take a leap of faith in the opinion of her friend Dawn, since she hadn't yet been to the cabin. She knew that, for this price, it would most certainly require work. But it was a risk she was willing to take as it appeared perfect from the pictures she had seen.

With just a few material possessions in her small car, Cassie began her journey to her new beginning—her new life. Roger gave her a heartfelt embrace as she packed the final piece of luggage into the back hatch and walked to the driver's door. As she drove away, she watched, tearfully, as Roger shrank and then disappeared from her rearview mirror. However, she knew that he most likely had been waving all the while.

She thought back to the day, now several years before, when a moving van had pulled up to the back door of Tammy and Steve's old home, and Cassie and Thad had watched reluctantly as Roger took over the one last possession that reminded them of their dear friends.

But over the years, Roger had grown to become such an important figure in their lives—and especially in Cassie's once Thad too was gone. She suddenly realized just how true a friend he had become, even when she hadn't thought that she needed one.

Cassie now realized that, though this relationship held little threat or promise of intimacy, Roger had become so important to her. Once the fog of recent widowhood had lifted a bit, she had found that Roger's friendship had become a priceless asset.

She appreciated everything he had done for her over the years, and she wondered if she was making a wise choice. Cassie hoped that he would be blessed with nice neighbors even though she had no clue as to the fate of the place she had known as home for so long. Roger, meanwhile, wished her the same happiness and realized just how much he would truly miss her.

Once she was no longer in sight, Roger tightly grasped the keys that she had left for him to give to the new owners. Cassie had known that relinquishing those items to the new owners would be too emotional for her, and Roger was eager to help.

Roger turned the front doorknob for what he suspected would be the last time and began to think back to memories of times spent together—good and bad. He recalled stories that she had shared during the initial months of her grief journey and the times that she had begun to learn how to laugh among her tears, especially when she would speak of Thad.

One particular story came flooding back to him, and now among his tears, he found himself laughing once more. Cassie had taken Thad to get a colonoscopy. She had sat in the waiting room of the medical facility, working on needlework while they proceeded with the exam. A while had passed, and a nurse came out to the waiting room, saying, "Mrs. Malone, the procedure is done and all is well. He is beginning to come out of the twilight sleep, and it shouldn't be long before you can take him home." Cassie had begun winding down on her project, packing things away so she would be ready to go whenever Thad was released.

Though she wasn't exactly sure how long she waited, Cassie had told Roger that it seemed like at least another hour went by without another word from anyone. Then suddenly, the same nurse walked back out to her, sat down, and began to explain, "Your husband woke up okay. But he went into the restroom to change clothes and apparently failed to lock the door. One of the other nurses walked in on him, not realizing that he was in there. She hit him in the head with the door, so we decided to lay him back down and keep him under observation for a little while longer, as we think that he possibly has a concussion."

In telling the story, Cassie had continued on with a slight chuckle, something Roger hadn't really witnessed in her lately. "Thad was the only man I ever knew who could go in for a colonoscopy and come out with a concussion," she continued amid her own laughter. Roger was always willing to listen to their stories, but this one was most certainly his favorite.

Roger finished up a bit of tidying and walked out the back door of the house to the path beaten flat by familiar footsteps. He wondered if it would be the last time he would be as welcomed in that house as Cassie had made him feel. He knew nothing at all about the new owners of Cassie's little house, and he hoped that they would be half the neighbors that the Malones had been.

Meanwhile, Cassie was well on her way to her new home. Filled with anticipation and intrigue, as well as a bit of anxiety, she really had little clue what she was going to find once she got there.

The overly packed vehicle approached the small town where she would now reside, and after a brief stop at the title company to sign a few documents, Cassie scooped up the keys. She then found herself driving down the gravel-paved, back-country road to her new home.

She was relieved that, for the most part, the documents for the sale of her old home had been done online, and she hadn't had to attend an actual closing. Cassie had felt concerned that a face-to-face closing could be a bit over-whelming for her, and the new owners had seemed more than willing to accommodate any requests she had made.

The final leg of her three-hour journey was now complete, and she had followed the last of the directions from the realtor to help her locate her new home. She had seen a few pictures of the place, and Dawn had described it to her detail by detail over the phone. But all things considered, neither the pictures nor Dawn had done it justice. As she turned onto the long and windy driveway and entered through the wooded gate that separated the property from the rest of the world, she was filled with joy and amazement—just before her stood an adorable little log cabin upon a stone foundation.

The front door swung open as she approached the top step of the front porch, and Cassie was pleased to meet the outreached arms of her new best friend, Dawn. It was even more of a pleasure when she realized that Dawn actually only lived a mile away, and since Dawn also no longer worked outside of her home, the two had already began conjuring up schemes for the days ahead. But for now, the two women had enough chores ahead as they began touring the log home and getting Cassie settled there.

The first marvel Cassie spotted was a stone fireplace that sat in the middle of a living room, surrounded by a winding staircase. Cassie recognized the mantle as a wonderful location for the anniversary clock that had rested upon the mantle in her previous home. She had often considered the prospect of taking it to a clock-repair shop as she had never been handy at fixing things. But she had never taken the time. Cassie felt that, in time, she would get it taken care of, though. For now, she would just appreciate its sight and think back if she wanted to appreciate its sound.

As she continued to scan the room, a loft overhead drew her attention. After a brief inspection of the kitchen, master bedroom, and two nicely sized bathrooms, Cassie felt excited about her new home. The cabin had an open floor plan, and living alone, she realized that it would work out nicely for her. It was very different from the home she had lived in with Thad, but different was what she desired now.

She proceeded to the back door to check out the view from the deck. She could only see trees and a babbling brook from where she stood as she glanced out over her half-acre yard. Wheels began spinning in her mind as she drew out potential landscaping options. Dawn, having witnessed the intense look on Cassie's face, piped up with, "I will help you build this up to a place you can relax and enjoy for years to come. Together we can make this place a haven."

Dawn realized that this was more than her friend had hoped for as a huge smile came across Cassie's face. It was obvious that Cassie felt that she had found a *new* place to call home.

Later that night, Cassie dozed, half a glass of wine still at her side, as she sat in front of the fireplace. Within, small embers still burned, remnants of her little celebration of her purchase. During the night, she awoke to see what she thought was a heart shape, illuminated within the burning embers that remained. But moments later, she fell back asleep and remained there for the rest of the night.

When she awoke again, the sun hung high in the sky, and the fire had extinguished itself. She realized that the heart had been a part of a dream and didn't give it another thought.

Just three days later, a moving van would approach the driveway and Cassie would begin to feel the full sense of her new life. But for now, she just felt like analyzing this new place she had bought, figuring out how to make it specifically hers.

*C*assie kept so busy with projects out in the yard for the first several months that she hardly realized she hadn't even bothered to get television or Internet service brought into the log cabin. But winter was approaching, and she knew that the yard projects would be ending for the year very soon.

Just two weeks later, Cassie and Dawn were sitting out back, enjoying one last fire for the year in the makeshift fire pit, sipping wine. "I am not sure what to do with my time now that winter is approaching," Cassie said.

"I was thinking about that." Dawn replied. "I know that you enjoy working in the yard, but the weatherman is predicting record snowfalls this year. I think it would do you good to find something to keep your mind occupied indoors this winter."

The next morning, bright and early, Cassie got on the phone and contacted the local Internet provider. She didn't even own a television anymore. Hers had been broken in the move, but she really didn't see that as a problem. She had only turned it on once since Thad died anyway. The one time she did try to watch, in an attempt to stay caught up on current events, the news had seemed to be focused on a crime boss who would soon come to trial after a major bust that had been made a few years ago.

Thad had now been gone for over a year, and since he had been ripped from her world, Cassie had spent most of her time finding new ways of keeping herself entertained. She discovered that changing her hobbies and interests made life easier to bear—now that she no longer had him by her side.

Her first attempt at trying something new was learning to play the piano. She bought a used baby grand and gave it her best effort, but she soon realized that it was not a good option for her. She had developed such a short attention span.

After several attempts at finding a new hobby, Cassie finally landed on something that seemed to fit her like a glove. She invested in a nice easel and a full array of paints and canvases. Whenever she needed to release emotions or just combat boredom, she would paint. It was actually an idea that Thad had planted in her head years before.

"Cassie, you are so creative. I think you should consider taking up painting or drawing...or something like that," Thad would tell her from time to time. She often would reply with a shrug, lacking the confidence to even try, and then turn and walk away from his request.

It wasn't until her job was no longer a part of her world that she realized how stressful it had been, all those years that she worked as a 9-1-1 operator. Looking back, she realized how difficult it would have been for her to focus on a project of this nature while working that job. But her world was completely different at this point.

After Thad was gone, the painting notion began crossing her mind occasionally, and she had actually begun to wonder if the idea was so far-fetched after all. She finally realized how right Thad had been.

Months went by, and Roger finally came to visit. He walked into her beautifully decorated cabin, and a tear once more trickled down his cheek as he observed the wonderful setting. Cassie gave him the grand tour, ending up on the loft to show him the beautiful view of the backyard, when he spotted her easel and the numerous paintings she had created since he had last seen her.

"I still wonder how he saw this in me for all of those years," Cassie told Roger as he looked, mesmerized, at her work. "Thad told me for so many years to give this painting thing a try. I generally just shrugged my shoulders and walked away whenever he mentioned it to me. How could he have possibly known?"

"You are really talented, Cassie. I had no idea," Roger said.

"This new hobby fits me like a glove. It was as if he knew me better than I knew myself sometimes," she continued.

He was amazed by the quality of the work. "What would you think about putting them on display?"

The very shy Cassie showed through as she replied, "Oh. you must be joking. You really think that other people would want to see these?"

"I have a very good friend back home that owns an art gallery. Would you mind if I show him some of your art?" he continued.

With slight reluctance at first, only because she couldn't recognize the beauty in what she had produced, she finally permitted him to place a call on her behalf. "I really don't feel that my work is gallery quality, but I trust your judgement. If you want to call your friend, I will entertain the idea at least," Cassie replied.

When the sun began to set, Roger acknowledged that it was time to make the journey back home. Home was nearly 150 miles away, and those back-country roads could be challenging at night. Roger gathered a few of Cassie's canvases and headed out the door to his SUV, making his way back home.

Days later, Cassie received a call. "Hi, Cassie. This is Bluford Davis from the Blue Ridge Art Gallery, but please call me Blu. Would you by any chance have more paintings that I could display in my gallery? I would like to create a wall of your works for an upcoming exhibition."

She could barely contain her excitement. Terrified that she would let too much emotion come out in her words, she choked out a simple, "Okay, I will bring what I have completed into the gallery tomorrow, if that's okay."

The next morning, she packed the car with several pieces of her artwork and dropped them off at the gallery.

In no time, she began receiving requests for more of her work, and the royalties began to roll in as her paintings became in high demand.

Cassie became overwhelmed with the outpouring of support from friends and strangers alike, as a newly discovered career took flight. Suddenly, she was finding little time for anything but painting. But that was, once again, a welcome distraction for her.

Seasons changed, and she began to really grow into this new role she found herself playing. Work was suddenly fun for her. She thought back to her former life, back to the days of solving problems and working with never-ending stressful situations. Now her work made her relax, which was a good thing, since it occupied so much of her time.

Cassie's paintings had become sought after in what felt like no time at all. It was as though the joy and pride she felt whenever she sold another painting soothed the ache she had been unable to eliminate before, since Thad's accident.

There had also grown a nearly immediate spark between Cassie and Blu. They shared a common interest, and she found him quite interesting. He had brought her into a completely new and exciting world.

Then one day, she answered her phone and heard something she'd never anticipated. Recognizing the number on the caller ID, she answered, "Good morning Blu," expecting more requests for paintings.

Blu replied with an energy that she had not previously witnessed from him. "Good morning to you too, Cassie. While I would have rather asked this in person, I find it difficult to get up the nerve when I see your face. What I was wondering is, would you consider going out to dinner with me sometime soon?"

She realized that he was not proposing a business meeting, and she replied in the only way she felt possible. In her heart, she still felt very married. "I sincerely appreciate the offer, but I am just not sure that I am in a position to start a new relationship."

"How about just dinner and let things happen as they may?"

She accepted, and in time, Cassie began dating the gallery owner. It was a difficult concept for her and she wondered what Thad would think of her new romance.

After months of trying to put her thoughts of Thad aside, Cassie realized that as hard as she tried, she just couldn't proceed with the relationship with Blu, and they parted as friends. However, he acknowledged her talent and continued to support and promote her career.

With the release of the relationship, Cassie felt once more the sting of heartache. She missed what they'd shared, but she never looked back. It had become clear to her that it was not the right time for anything more than a friendship. It remained a strong one, but it never again became anything more.

She began submerging herself in work once more. Now that she had Internet at her home, whenever she was between paintings or just needed to take a break from them, she spent time on various social-media sites. She and Thad had spent quite a bit of time on them during the last several years of their marriage, and they had developed a rather extensive list of online contacts.

Now with her paintings in the forefront of her mind, she tried to expand her audience even more, in order to keep everyone back home informed of her shows and such. By this time, Cassie had made quite a name for herself in the artistic arena. She knew that she had a reason to be proud.

ven with her newfound successes, Cassie continued to feel that something was missing. So on a
typical Monday morning in midspring, as she and
Dawn sat out on the back deck sipping coffee, Cassie mentioned that void. She also revealed a little secret about her
work: "If you hold each of my paintings in just a certain
way under a black light, you will see an illuminated heart
in them. It's just one more signature that I chose to give
to my paintings. It gives me the inspiration to continue,
as if Thad's spirit is here with me."

It had been a little over three years since they had sat
together on the plane, and in that time, Dawn had listened to many stories. They usually resulted in laughter
or tears, whichever mood fitted the moment.

"Cassie, I completely understand your sense of emptiness," Dawn replied. "As you know full well, I never
had the opportunity to meet Thad. But you have shared
so much of your life with him in the stories you've told
me that I can't help but feel that I did. I have personally
watched you build a success out of a mere coping mecha-
nism when you first moved here." She continued com-
passionately, "I have no doubt that Thad would want you
to find happiness in this world any way you can."

"Thanks, Dawn. I know you are right," she replied
sheepishly. But the truth was, Cassie had no idea what
would truly make her happy. However, she did take
Dawn's words to heart, and more soul-searching began.

That evening, after Dawn had left for home, Cassie
began spending a little time on the social-media sites,
even visiting Thad's profile page. Cassie had never had
the heart to shut it down, and she really felt that it would
serve no purpose to do so. She herself had been known
to stop by the wall and post a note to him, mostly on special days, as if heaven too had Internet. Who was she to
question—maybe it did. She would then read posts from
others who must have felt the same.

One day as she scrolled through Thad's social-media
sites, she decided to open a folder that, by default, accepted
messages from strangers. She had sorted through hundreds

of old posts that day, from game requests from people Thad had met playing his online games, to girls offering to assist him in finding pleasure in his life, to well wishes from old friends who hoped Cassie would find their kind words. Cassie knew not to be offended by the various types of spam that she had found in this folder. She received those on her profile page as well, and it was meaningless junk. But as she skimmed the message folder, one particular message seemed to call out to her. So she opened it and began to read. It was from a man who claimed to have known Thad during his days in the army: "I know this is not Thad reading this message. Cassie, I have heard of his passing and am truly saddened. He was a great man, and I would feel honored to be accepted as a friend to you, his widow."

Thad had served a short stint before she had met him. They hadn't talked of his experiences much, so she had a limited amount to add to any stories this man might share, but the idea intrigued her. She could possibly learn about another side of Thad from this man.

Her new Internet stranger, Larry, became a great early-morning distraction for her. He had been a little mysterious regarding his whereabouts, but that didn't seem to matter much. She was drawn to him because he was one of very few who could relate to her on a particular level. He had known Thad as a young man, something she didn't share with many at this stage of her life.

While she had found some satisfaction from sharing stories about Thad with Dawn, it was difficult for her to find anyone to "compare notes" with about Thad, as it seemed that most of their mutual friends no longer walked the earth.

Some days she and Larry would sit and chat online for hours. Larry had so many stories about the Thad she had never gotten the chance to know. Cassie was happy to have a new friend—and a link to the man she had missed so much for the past few years.

Months of daily online chats later, Cassie felt comfortable in making a request to Larry. "Would you allow me to friend you on my own account?" she asked. He had never asked, and she wondered if he was just shy or if there was another reason.

"I would rather we just continue messaging the way we do. I am not really the social-media type," Larry replied. It didn't seem that strange to her. They had been chatting for so long now, and she felt she could trust him.

This brought about a new realization for her. Cassie had begun to trust a man other than Thad in a way she had never considered before. Up to this point, her husband had been the only man she had ever allowed to hold that special part of her heart. She recalled how Blu had tried but failed. Overall, she felt that it was most likely never going to happen for her again.

Cassie realized that she had to accept the fact that she was falling in love with Larry—and she knew it. She struggled with the concept, thinking that maybe she was just feeling this closeness because he had been her link back to the man she had adored for so much of her life. Cassie held back from revealing her true feelings. At times it almost felt as if she were tied to a chair, sitting on her hands. But she resisted her urges and offered him a simple "Good day." She wondered how long she could hold back, knowing that she needed to tell him of her feelings.

But they had never even spoken of his love interests. She knew so very little of his personal life, and he seemed to want to keep it that way. He had no pictures on his virtual wall, at least none that she was permitted to see, and just a limited supply of friends. As online chatting friends, she felt safe talking with him, although he was making no effort to take the relationship anywhere else. She was willing to accept this, however, even if friendship were all that would ever take place. She was just glad to have a friend who was capable of telling her new stories of Thad. At least that was what Cassie would tell herself.

pring soon turned to summer, and summer to
fall. Cassie found herself once more preparing for
an art exhibit at the Blue Ridge Art Gallery, the
place where her career had begun. She had not seen its
owner for quite some time and considered that it might
be awkward when the two met face to face once more. She
hadn't even thought of him for over a year now, and while
she hoped all was well in his world, she knew that what
they had shared was not what she would ever need again.

Cassie had been happy just having her online chat
friend to fill her days, to fill an emptiness that no one
else had come close to filling in her years of grieving.

Then one day it happened—Cassie let her feelings
slip to Larry. She informed him that she had fallen in

love with him and that she wondered if they could meet. Her heart sank a bit as she read his reply:

"Cassie, I am a married man. While I feel strongly about our friendship, I am so very much in love with my wife. Our relationship is complicated, and I guess I reached out to you in a time of desperation and loneliness. But make no mistake, she is the reason my sun rises in the morning. I never intended to allow this to become more than just what it is. I want nothing more than to continue our talks but fear that a meeting would not be a good idea at this time. She owns my heart and my soul."

At first Cassie tried to conceal her immense disappointment, but she soon found that the chats had to end. It saddened her so, but she knew that it was for the best.

Cassie continued to prepare for exhibits. While the quality of her work remained constant, the style changed after this friendship ended. There was one particular piece in her next collection that, in retrospect, she wished she'd never created. It was unlike anything she had ever done. It reflected the moment when she realized that she had fallen for her online friend.

Cassie had always written a message on the backs of her canvases, mostly in an attempt to explain her thoughts during each particular creative process. This piece was only different in the respect that her hidden message was quite lengthy and much more heartfelt than any other she had written ever before—almost poetic.

The painting itself had been an abstract of her broken heart. But more importantly, it contained so much of her intimate thoughts on the back and Cassie wasn't comfortable with anyone else reading her words. She had intended to keep this painting to herself, but it had accidentally been sent on to the gallery, and she hoped she could retrieve it before someone else took ownership. She really didn't want anyone else to see just how deeply her heart had fallen for Larry or how much it still ached for Thad. She recalled the words she'd scrawled across the back of the canvas:

One Random Day

I awoke from grief's coma and realized that there was so much wrong in my world—in my house!

So I called a dear friend to assist. We marched through the house, with clipboard in hand, as I analyzed what my home was lacking. I stated each and every thing that I wanted to change before I came to the conclusion that I no longer wanted to reside there alone. So a search began. My heart took me to a looking point, a place where I could at least temporarily survive.

Then, one random day...

I decided to check an online site. I sorted through several houses and much to my surprise, one house appealed to me. At first I wasn't able to open the door. I couldn't see what it looked like inside, but I liked the parts I could see.

So I made a leap of faith and made it mine. I opened the front door and began to realize...

This house that had mysteriously pulled me in from afar contained every little thing my old home was missing. It was as though a prayer had been answered, though I didn't even remember making the request.

So I reached through the computer screen and pulled it in. Soon my heart decided that I could reside there.

The pages of the calendar flipped several times. I awoke again from grief's coma and realized that there was so much wrong in my world—in my heart!

So I called a dear friend to assist. We searched my heart, with clipboard in hand, as I analyzed what my soul was lacking. I stated each and every thing that I wanted to change before I came to the conclusion that I no longer wanted to reside there alone. So a search began. My soul took me to a looking point, a place where I could at least temporarily survive.

Then, one random day...

I decided to check a message folder. I sorted through several well wishes from unknown people, and much to my surprise, one message appealed to me. At first I didn't open the message. I couldn't see what it looked like inside, but I liked the parts I could see.

So I made a leap of faith and made it mine. I opened the note and begin to realize...

The message that had mysteriously pulled me in from afar contained a simple request asking me to be his friend. It was as though a prayer had been answered, though I didn't even remember making the request.

So I reached through my computer screen and pulled him in. Soon my soul decided that it could reside there.

When Cassie realized that this deeply personal piece had been sent with the others for her showing, Cassie immediately called Blu.

"Oh, Cassie, I am so sorry, but that particular piece has already been sold. In fact, you have quite an avid admirer of your work. I've been meaning to tell you this. It seems to be the same person, a woman, who left a number on file. She has requested that I contact her prior to every one of your exhibits. Everything is done over the Internet. I have never met her, but she buys much of your work, some even sight unseen," Blu told her. He also stated that it had been made clear to him from the start that the buyer wanted to remain anonymous, even to the artist. Since the buyer always paid the full asking price and was diligent with her payment, he felt that it was in Cassie's best interest, or at least the best interest of her career, to oblige.

It pained her to think that she had let her heart be so exposed on her canvas. Cassie knew that she should have never allowed those words to leave her heart. The thought that they now hung, though hidden from potential viewers by coats of paint, upset her. She had to accept that it most likely now hung up on some collector's wall. She resigned herself to the fact that she had little or no options here, and she had learned through her grief process to release the things that she was unable to change.

As predicted, winter hit hard, and Cassie found herself quite relieved that Dawn lived within walking distance. She had been so busy following her heart, building her art career, that she hadn't spent much time getting to know anyone else. As she sat one evening in front of a warm fire, wine glass in hand and a true friend sitting at the other end of the cozy seating area, Cassie began bouncing ideas off Dawn, ideas of what she could do to fill a void that had once more entered her heart.

"I realize that I have limited my contact with others. I just get so wrapped up in my work. But I also am aware that I am happier when I maintain some form of human contact. I guess it's time to think about doing something that gets me out of this cabin once in a while," Cassie confessed.

"I'm glad to see that you have realized this, Cassie. Have you ever thought about volunteering somewhere?" Dawn asked.

"I do think about that sometimes. I have been given so many great opportunities over the years, and now that I have a successful career, I often feel like maybe it's time I consider giving something back," Cassie replied.

At the end of the discussion, they both concluded that maybe she should offer her services as a volunteer at an orphanage.

Cassie didn't waste time when she made up her mind to do something. She set things up and immediately began doing what she did best: she spent one day each week teaching children at a nearby orphanage how to express themselves through art. In time, she got to know several of the children quite well. But one girl approaching womanhood drew her in, capturing a part of Cassie's heart that she had been determined to keep closed off from the rest of the world.

Treasa had lived at the orphanage since being abandoned as an infant. Apparently she had been left at the orphanage after being discovered on a windy spring afternoon, resting unattended in an old derelict car in an empty parking lot. Cassie wasn't sure what it was about the young girl that brought them so close, but she wasn't going to fight the urge to get to know her better.

Cassie considered becoming a foster parent, feeling that maybe she could be there for other children who needed a home, bringing herself back to those feelings of neglect and diminished self-worth she had encountered in her young life. But with her career at what seemed to be an uphill swing, she soon realized that it wouldn't be in the best interest of any child. But it didn't stop her from building a strong bond with Treasa as she maintained her volunteer status at the home.

Even though the time she spent online had reduced, Cassie still logged on once in a while. Over time, other anonymous requests for friendships would appear. But she couldn't get past the hurt she'd felt when she realized how she had allowed herself to get sucked in by her feelings for Larry. She had vowed at the end of their friendship never again to accept any such requests. She still would receive an occasional "Hi, how ya doing?" from him. But she would resist temptation to send a reply.

Cassie missed her talks with Larry but felt that her heart just couldn't survive another loss. This was not up for debate, in her mind; she had to move on and stop thinking about him. She realized this but found it to be easier said than done.

Six months later, Cassie admitted to herself that nothing but painting could keep her interests for long. She decided to step away from her volunteer work and begin traveling once more. Cassie recalled that trip she had made several years ago, when she first met Dawn. This time she didn't leave it up to fate, though. She made plans to visit the mountains in order to obtain inspiration by viewing their majesty.

Cassie realized that a month in Sedona, Arizona, could refresh her to once more attempt to create artistic masterpieces. Blu had been telling her that her biggest fan, the anonymous purchaser, had been contacting him again, looking for more hangings. But she had realized that her motivation had dwindled, and she suspected that an unfamiliar setting would be the perfect muse. Cassie decided not to make the trip alone, so Dawn once more boarded the same plane, but this time it was more than merely a coincidence.

During the month's visit, they enjoyed the splendor the area offered. A trip to the Grand Canyon summed up the trip just one day before they boarded the plane back home. Dawn had witnessed its vastness and beauty once before, as a small child. But for Cassie, growing up in the orphanage in Missouri, her experiences had been extremely limited.

The return plane ride was as uneventful as the trip out had been, something they viewed as a good thing where flying was concerned.

The two women had mailed many souvenirs back home before leaving to avoid buying another suitcase to get all of their belongings home. Upon landing back at the airport, they gathered their mass of luggage from baggage carousel A and then wearily made their way to the long-term parking garage that had hosted Cassie's car for the better part of the month.

Arriving home completely exhausted, Cassie failed to notice the package resting on the wooden bench on her front porch. She began clearing the evidence that Mother Nature had visited her home while she was away, shovel in hand, making a path to allow passage from the driveway to the porch steps; suddenly she noticed this package.

At first she figured that some of their vacation purchases had beaten them home. But she opened it to find a chain adorned with a simple heart-shaped pendant. As she looked closer, she noticed that it also contained a stone in the middle of the heart—her birthstone. It was a mystery. Who had sent it? It didn't contain a card or any-thing to indicate where it had come from. It was clear that the package had been personally placed there by someone who had stopped by her home during her absence. It had not been dropped off by any form of mail service, that much was evident.

Her first thoughts were of Larry. This almost an-gered her to think that he would send her a gift. The wrap looked like it had been intended for Valentine's Day as the package was concealed in red-and-white tissue, completed by the accent of a beautifully tied white bow. But then she remembered that she had never exchanged addresses with him. He would have had no way to find her; she was quite certain of that.

Her next thought was Roger. "No, sweetie, I didn't send you a gift for Valentine's Day," Roger said when she asked him. "It would have been a nice thought, and I wish I had, but I can't take credit for the thoughtfulness of someone else. Maybe Blu or Tim sent it to you. Have you asked them?"

Realizing how uncharacteristic such behavior would have been from either of them, her thoughts went im-mediately back to Larry.

She had divulged so many intimate details to him during their daily chats all those months ago, and he knew the significance the heart shape held for her. But he had made his feelings clear to her and the idea of receiving such a gift from him was just not appropriate. The more she looked at and thought about the gift, the angrier she became. If it was a gift from Larry, that was just cruel!

Memories of her life with Thad came flooding back. Cassie's mind wandered back to that early April morning, decades ago, when that tractor trailer had parked illegally in front of her home, and she became his for what she thought would be a lifetime. But lifetime with him had been cut short, and she tried most days to keep that part of her memory shut off. It was just too painful to remember—still! She couldn't help but feel that this gift was just a rotten joke sent to her by someone, causing her to miss Thad all over again.

nce the anger subsided a bit, Cassie began creating beautiful artwork once more. She even considered talking to Blu about setting up another exhibit. But she realized that her inventory of completed works was nowhere near enough to accommodate the demand, so she put every ounce of energy she had into her work. She seemed to surround herself in a cocoon, filled with paint and canvas, not even taking time to have those ever-so-important daily chats with Dawn that she had grown to appreciate over the years since she'd moved into the cabin.

Time flew quickly while she engrossed herself in her projects, and one day Cassie realized that she had enough paintings completed to warrant a trip, so she loaded them up and took them to the gallery. Blu, having not laid eyes upon her beauty in quite some time, welcomed her by wrapping his sturdy arms about her petite frame. He swept her up and swung her around, and she noticed a change in him. It was apparent to her that he had missed her and even possibly had the desire to rekindle a flame that had died for her a long time ago.

"I have been thinking a lot of you, over the past several months especially. I hadn't heard anything from you in what seemed like forever. I've missed you," he said.

She had tossed her feelings for him away long ago and had no intention of entertaining that relationship ever again. Cassie politely told him that and saw a hidden sadness in his eyes unlike anything she had ever seen there before. But it was not going to happen for them again, and she felt it best to not lead him on.

She suddenly thought back to the heart pendant.

Over the years, Cassie had acquired an outspoken air about her, and she fully intended to implement that here with her old friend. "I want to ask you something. I received a heart-shaped pendant for Valentine's Day. Did you send it to me?" she asked.

He replied with an emphatic no.

Once the car was unloaded, she turned away from Blu's broken heart once more and made her journey home.

As she began her drive, she chose to take the path less traveled rather than the interstate, which had become her typical route. During this trip, she reflected back to a memory that had sunk so far into the recesses of her mind that she barely recognized its source. Why had Thad suddenly entered her thoughts again? She had worked so hard to overcome that loss, and she'd thought that she had moved fully into her new life. But she now realized that occasionally he would still cross her mind.

Cassie decided to turn off from her intended route, just as she approached the road leading to the home she and Thad had lived in together. The house still stood, almost untouched, and the sight was more than she could bear. So instead of stopping to visit Roger, she decided to call him from her car phone instead. They had a brief but pleasant conversation as he was running late for work.

Another mystery appeared as she pulled into the driveway of her cabin. She was surprised to see a beautiful young woman standing next to a modest compact car parked in front of her garage door. Cassie pulled in alongside and was filled with excitement as she realized who this woman was. Treasa from the orphanage was now a woman out on her own in the real world. Cassie ran to her and reached out her arms, pulling her in tightly.

"Oh, Treasa. I can't believe it's you. I am so sorry that I haven't kept in touch with you better. I guess I got really wrapped up in my work," Cassie admitted.

"Cassie, it's okay. I understand, but I have missed you," Treasa replied.

After sharing several cups of coffee, Cassie extended the offer for Treasa to stay with her for a while, and Treasa graciously accepted the warm invitation.

Cassie cleared a corner of the loft that had become crowded with her art supplies over the past years, in an attempt to make room for her guest. Treasa didn't seem to mind a bit. "I can sleep on the floor if nothing else. I'm just grateful for the roof over my head and the time to spend with the one person who felt more like a parent to me over the years than anyone else."

Cassie had already had a rather emotional day, and hearing those words took her thoughts away for a moment, back to the couple who had made her feel that same way years ago. But thoughts of Tammy and Steve now left her with a warm feeling—remembering how much they had loved her like a daughter.

Although her face-to-face visits with Treasa had drastically reduced once Cassie had stopped volunteering, Cassie had seen to it that Treasa received a gift for every birthday and Christmas that passed, ever since the very beginning of their acquaintance.

Where there had once been a twosome for morning coffee, consisting of Cassie and Dawn, they easily found room at the table and in their hearts for Treasa. Some days, it ended up just being two, though, whenever Dawn's schedule became too hectic. She had taken a job as a waitress at a local restaurant, claiming that she had found herself falling on hard times. But the chair would sit empty, waiting for the next chance for the three of them to share any new developments in their lives.

One such morning, with Dawn at work, Cassie could see that Treasa was concerned about something, just by looking into the young girl's eyes.

"What is wrong, Treasa?" she asked, stammering a bit before getting the words to leave her mouth.

"You know that I kind of think of you as a mom, right?" Treasa replied.

Cassie nodded in acknowledgement and agreement.

"But I feel the need to find out where I come from. How would you feel if I began a search for my birth mother?" Treasa continued.

Being an orphan as well, something that she had never informed Treasa of in all the years she'd known her, Cassie completely understood, and she even offered to assist in any way she could.

The only information they had to begin their search was the location of that old car where Treasa had been found abandoned. They drove to the police station with jurisdiction over that area and began to ask questions. No one seemed to want to offer much assistance, however.

The women left discouraged, but they did leave contact information with the hopes that someone might be willing to offer help.

everal days later there was a knock at Cassie's front
door. She recognized the face of the man as having been at the police station when they had been
discussing Treasa's search, days ago. She opened the door
and the slovenly dressed, large-framed older gentleman
addressed her.

"Ms. Malone?" the detective questioned.

"Yes, I am Mrs. Malone. What can I help you with?"

"I am Detective Peterson. I was at the police station
the other day when you came in with a young girl."

She offered him entrance into her home and proceeded into the kitchen, where they sat down at a small

table that stood in the corner. Cassie offered him a cup of coffee, and the two began to talk about Treasa. As the story he shared began to unfold, Cassie was relieved that Treasa had decided to spend the day in town at the orphanage, trying to see if there was any information to be uncovered there.

Detective Peterson began by telling her about a troubling case in his unsolved folder for several years, and how he had just recently stumbled across its resolution. It seemed that a young woman had turned up missing, along with her newborn child. She had been a single mother with no family to speak of, with the exception of her estranged adoptive family. It seemed that the girl had been a college student at a nearby university when she discovered that she was pregnant. When the couple who raised her had discovered the news, they refused to offer her any more assistance and the young girl had been left to make a life for her soon-to-arrive child all on her own. Just weeks after the baby arrived, she had been reported missing when she didn't show up for any of her classes following an extended weekend.

Detective Peterson had been assigned that case. Up to this point in his career, he had held a rather impressive record. But this case had him baffled. The family seemed uninterested, which had always concerned the detective, but he could never find any evidence linking them to her disappearance. The detective told Cassie that several of the missing young woman's fellow students had informed him that she had kept pretty much to herself. They remarked how this had especially been the case when she returned for this semester, shortly after she had given birth. There was even concern that she had begun hanging out with a bad crowd, with her showing signs of drug usage.

He concluded by telling Cassie that this young girl's remains had recently been found, badly decomposed, along with what was left of an old camera, lying at the bottom of a roadside cliff. Upon further investigation, it was ruled accidental. She must have stopped to take a picture and slid on some loose rocks.

The case has now finally, after all these years, been marked as closed. Something always had troubled him about the case, however. While several of the girl's classmates had indicated that she had recently given birth, he had never been able to locate a child—until now. At least that's what he had begun to suspect.

The detective's newly uncovered research had indicated that the infant had been brought to a shelter or orphanage and left there by a homeless man, who apparently had claimed, in a note attached to her blanket, that he had heard the little one crying from the back of an unattended vehicle. Detective Peterson had suspected that this very same homeless man had also taken it upon himself to remove the plates and steal the car on that day. His theory had been confirmed when he found what looked to be a rusty old license plate not far from where the body had been found.

Cassie was not at all sure how to relay this information to Treasa. But she knew that the girl needed to know that her search may have not been entirely in vain, even if it wasn't exactly what she had hoped to find.

Cassie had grown to feel so much like a mother to the girl since they'd first met, but she also realized that it would cause the young woman's heart to break, at least a little. Cassie wanted nothing more than to spare her the pain of losing a loved one, even if it was someone she had basically never met. Cassie had dealt with so much loss already in her life, and she wasn't quite sure how she could break the girl's heart this way. She soon realized that it might be beneficial to have Dawn there as well when she broke the news to Treasa.

Cassie excused herself for a moment to place a call. She picked up the phone, and within minutes, her best friend was as her front door. Not long after, the detective took leave, and the two women began figuring out the best way to tell Treasa the news.

Moments later the cabin door swung open, and Cassie could see by the look in Treasa's eyes that she had not been successful in her task.

"Well, that was a waste of time," Treasa remarked, disgusted, as she stormed into the kitchen.

Dawn pulled out a chair and motioned for the young girl to sit. "Sweetie, why don't you sit here with us for a bit? We need to talk about something."

Treasa seemed to recognize the distressed looks on the women's faces as she slowly took her seat next to them.

"I had a visit from a police detective a bit ago," Cassie began. "He had some information about a woman he suspects was your mother."

Cassie continued to tell her the story that Detective Peterson had shared.

At first, the news hit the girl very hard. But then she realized that, while one door had closed, another had possibly just opened. She now had discovered that, first of all, she had not just been left unloved for strangers to care for, but that her mom was most likely gone from her world. She figured that was why she had been left all of those years ago, and that thought gave her a sense of peace.

Secondly, she realized that, while her mother's adoptive parents had made a poor decision when they'd turned their backs on her and her mother all those years ago, Treasa did have a place to go to find out more about the woman who had given birth to her.

A phone call back to the detective two days later gave the girls their next focal point. The detective reluctantly gave them the names of Treasa's mother's adoptive parents but also advised them of two things: "First of all, I must tell you, they didn't seem very concerned about her well-being then. Please don't get your hopes up. And secondly, they weren't exactly young then. It's quite possible that they are no longer living."

But along with the warnings, he also gave them an address and phone number that he had written down in the case file so long ago. They had left him with such an uncaring impression that when this case had been recently closed, he hadn't even given second thought to attempting to contact them to let them know. He truly felt that they didn't really care.

These were bitter words to befall Treasa's ears, and Cassie could see the tears welling up in the corners of her precious eyes. But she also knew that it wasn't as much about reconnecting with family as it had been about discovering where she came from. So the two climbed into the car and headed back to what Cassie soon discovered were all-too-familiar roads. It turned out that the couple who had taken Treasa's mom into their home so many years before actually lived just across the river from the orphanage where a much younger Cassie had spent her childhood.

Cassie began to wonder if she had shared any time together with Treasa's mother at the orphanage when they were children. It seemed quite possible to her that they would have been close in age. After all, she was the right age to have been Treasa's mother given different circumstances.

When they pulled up in front of the little white bungalow, nervousness began to set in. Now, for very different reasons, both Cassie and Treasa had purposes for being there.

"Are you sure that you really want to do this?" Cassie asked.

"Yes, Cassie. I need to know where I came from. You have been so great to me over these past couple of years, but this is something I feel I must do," Treasa replied.

The two walked through the arbor and up the shrub-lined sidewalk to the front door. Neither of them could have possibly been prepared for what they were about to discover as they knocked timidly on that front door.

A middle-aged woman answered—far too young to be Treasa's adoptive grandparents—and the two immediately realized that the detective may have been right about the couple being no longer living.

"I am sorry, but we were looking for the couple who would have lived here about twenty years ago," Cassie began.

With that, a frail voice echoed out from the next room: "Lucy, who is it?"

The woman standing with door knob in hand replied, "It's a couple of women, and I believe they might be looking for you, Mrs. Lavour."

There was a sharp quality in the voice coming from the next room, but also an underlying warmth. "Ask them to come in and have a seat in the living room. I will get up and join them if you will come and help me."

The house smelled of mothballs and musk. They sat down on the plastic-covered couch, which, while reminiscent of something you would have seen in a furniture store showroom back fifty years ago, still looked brand new, as if it had never been touched by human skin. The two sat there for quite some time as the woman who had answered the door left to assist the elderly woman whom they were anxiously awaiting to meet.

With a walker for support and a shawl wrapped tightly about her, the woman stumbled her way into the room, the woman who was apparently her nurse holding her elbow. With much help from her assistant, the woman firmly planted herself in a chair directly across the room from Cassie and Treasa.

W hat happened next took both Cassie and Treasa by complete surprise. They watched the old woman as tears suddenly formed in her eyes.

"Oh my, you look so much like Angie," she said.

Cassie and Treasa remembered the detective stating that the missing girl's name had been Angela Lavour.

Treasa replied with an excited voice, something that Cassie hadn't seen from her lately, "I look like my mom?"

Mrs. Lavour responded, "Not you—her." She pointed weakly toward Cassie. "You must be Cassie."

A sense of complete shock came over Cassie. "Would you please explain?"

"You were a toddler when we picked up your baby sister from the orphanage. I wanted to take you both, but Fred insisted that I must choose only one of you girls," she said as a steady stream of tears began to flow. "You seemed so withdrawn, and you cried so much. With both of you still in diapers, Mr. Lavour felt that it might be too much to take care of you both. It was a difficult decision, but I had to do as he asked."

How could she have forgotten that she had a baby sister? She had known during her years in the orphanage that the shock of losing her parents, combined with the trauma of the accident itself, had left her stricken. But she had no idea it had affected her so badly.

With jaw dropped, Cassie replied, "But we are here on behalf of her," pointing to Treasa, who appeared completely stunned by this revelation.

"And who are you, miss?" Mrs. Lavour asked.

Treasa replied, sounding almost questioning, "I am Treasa. I suspect that I am Angie's daughter. The detective told me that my mom lived here before she went away to college."

What had before been just a steady flow of tears now turned into hysterical bawling by Mrs. Lavour. The nurse got up and walked quickly toward the door. "I think it would be best if you two leave now," she stated. "Mrs. Lavour needs her rest, and you girls have upset her enough for one day."

Mrs. Lavour reached out her hands to grasp theirs as they made their way toward the door. "Please come again soon," she said through her tears.

Cassie and Treasa remained quiet as they made the trip back to the cabin. They were still struggling with the significance of the revelation that had just taken place. For the first time in both of their lives, they had family— real, true, blood-related family!

As they neared the driveway, Cassie failed to slow down the vehicle and just continued to drive on. Minutes later, she put the gearshift into park as they landed themselves directly in front of Dawn's home. Still not a word was uttered between the two. They just didn't know what to say, much less how to say it. The silence resonated, and the car engine seemed to sound louder than usual with no conversation to drown it out.

Dawn, realizing how peculiar it was that they had driven to her house rather than heading straight home, walked out to meet them as they approached her house.

"What is wrong?" Dawn asked. Cassie appeared nearly comatose as she all but walked right through her, as if she didn't see Dawn standing there, let alone hear the words she was speaking.

The three of them walked in and grabbed the first available seats, not worrying in the least about comfort. Dawn's unexpected visitors seemed stunned, as if they didn't even know how to begin talking about the events of the day. She had known where they were going and was now imagining the worst.

"Please, somebody tell me what is going on here," she pleaded.

With that, Treasa replied: "She's my aunt."

At first Dawn was uncertain of who *she* was. Then Cassie raised her hand in an attempt to clear up the confusion.

While you could have picked Dawn's chin up from the floor in front of her, she was at least still capable of speech. "This is a good thing—isn't it?"

Cassie, finally regaining the ability to speak, said, "Yes, it's remarkable. I have family."

It was at that exact moment that Dawn realized the magnitude of this situation. These two girls had lived their entire lives knowing that they had no one to call family. They had created a bond of friendship so strong that they felt as though they were a family. And now, with just a few spoken words from an elderly woman, they had found everything their former selves had been lacking. Their hearts had been filled with joy of the discovery, but at the same time, they had been completely caught off guard.

Later they would laugh of how their speechlessness must have been a family trait, but for now, it was just all far too new and unpredictable for them to discuss.

*C*assie awoke the following morning with many thoughts rushing through her head. She was not the only child she had grown up thinking she was, and she had not been left alone in this world without family.

Of course, Thad had certainly been her family. But when he'd died, she had worked hard to make herself realize that family was not something she would ever truly have again. Now she had a niece, along with the knowledge of a sister she had never really known. The first thing she intended to accomplish as her feet hit the floor that morning was to convince Treasa to make her cabin a permanent home, at least as permanent as a girl her age could accept.

The newly discovered family sat down to a light breakfast as they discussed possible events for the day. "I realize that you don't have a real room in this small cabin, Treasa. It would mean so much to me if you could feel comfortable enough to make this your home. I realize that we have never really discussed you actually living here permanently, even though you have been here for a while now. I am prepared to have an addition added onto the back if that's what it takes to get you to stay."

Treasa's eyes filled with tears. She had become overtaken by emotion as she began to feel the full effect of having someone to call family. She wasn't about to make her aunt go to a lot of trouble on her behalf. But she wasn't about to leave either.

Dawn had called Cassie the night before, just before retiring to bed for the night to make sure everyone was feeling better.

"I am so sorry that I was so distant yesterday. I just never imagined that I would ever find true family, let alone discover that *she* could be living right under my very own roof," Cassie said, thanking Dawn for her concern. "We are both doing fine."

But Dawn realized that it might be best for them to have a few days alone together. "I'll stop by over the weekend," she said just before she hung up the phone.

Days later, without another word about the cabin addition having been exchanged, Treasa was awoken abruptly by the sounds of hammers and saws. A construction crew had begun building an addition onto the back of the cabin. Cassie didn't believe in wasting much time, once she made a decision. This was no exception.

On day three of construction, Treasa decided to make a batch of cookies in order to offer the crew a homemade treat. With lemonade in one hand and the plate of cookies in the other, she approached the workers. Cassie had noticed a twinkle in her niece's eye when she'd spotted the youngest crew member the afternoon before. So the offering of this hospitality didn't surprise her in the least.

Drew was a towering, six-foot-tall, well-built construction worker. At least that was how it appeared as he stood next to the young girl's petite frame. But as Cassie watched from the kitchen window, she saw a definite spark between the two of them, and it did her heart good to watch from afar as this new friendship was formed. It took her back to a time, so many years ago, when her knight in shining armor had put her needs above his own and pulled over along that stretch of road and changed her life.

Cassie realized, once more, just how much she still missed Thad. It had been years since she had felt his touch, and she longed for that feeling just once more. Then she thought back to Larry. How could she have been so fooled by him? She thought he had wanted her as much as she had grown to realize she needed him. But his words *I am married...*echoed in her heart still. She had felt a familiarity with him, one that she had trusted to be more than just the sharing of stories between two people about a man who had been her world years ago.

She shook her head as though her brain were an Etch A Sketch. She longed to erase the pain she had endured over the years, but she desired to keep the memories themselves. Cassie knew that after all of these years, that may not be an option for her. But she was still willing to try.

She searched the deep recesses of her memory until she found a story that her mind could safely relive. Cassie thought back to a trip that had taken her away from Thad for a few days. She had been sent to attend a seminar in Chicago, hours and miles away from anyone she knew. Realizing the unfamiliarity of her present location, she had found herself a little ill at ease. While she was much more outgoing than Thad had been, this was one area that he excelled in comparison to her. He could always feel comfortable in strange places, while new places brought out the more reserved side of her, a side she rarely exposed. But this one particular fall day, as she was approaching the end of what felt like a very long week, a smile had begun to reform as she toted her first load of luggage out to the small SUV she and Thad had owned at the time.

With her suitcase strap tightly grasped in one hand and the handle of her rolling bag in the other, she reached into her pocket to pull out her keys. Suddenly a sound jolted her mind and made her feel a bit uneasy: the panic alarm blaring on one of the vehicles parked in the lot. She soon realized that the lights were flashing on her vehicle. Cassie realized that she must have hit the panic button as she pulled the keys from her pocket. So she pressed the button and the sound halted. But that was not the end of it. Although she carefully held the keys in her hand so as not to repeat the process, the lights began flashing once more as the sound recurred. Again she did what she had to do to make it stop. This happened a total of six times before she began hearing roaring laughter coming from the bushes not far away, as a very proud Thad with a matching remote revealed himself from the other side.

On one hand, she'd wanted to strangle Thad, but she couldn't help but laugh too. What were the odds that his delivery for that particular day, at that exact time, had been so close to where she had been staying for those past several days? While they had often laughed together at the recollection of that day, it seemed to tickle her much more now; she almost could feel his presence, as though they were reliving it together once more.

Cassie had accepted that she'd had something many never even come close to finding, and she had no right to feel self-pity that she might never have that again—with anyone. But she was happy to see Treasa smiling, and she hoped that true love may have found the young girl who stood before her now.

The workday ended for the construction crew, and the project was nearing completion. Treasa's smile began to fade. The workmen began loading tools into the back of their trucks, and Treasa realized that Drew was about to leave, and she might never see him again.

Inside, Treasa's mind continued to wander in thought of this man who had won her heart, when suddenly she heard a knock at the door. Her smile returned as she turned the knob to reveal who stood on the other side.

"Treasa, would you allow me to call you sometime?" asked the young man, who now appeared almost shy. He had not acted that way during their playful banter of the previous days, and she found his timidity quite appealing—and at the same time, amusing.

Unsure of whether she should risk continuing with the playfulness of days before, in light of his nearly panicked demeanor, she chose to reply with a quick smile and a simple yes.

They finished putting the last of their tools away, and the truck became smaller and smaller in her sight.

Treasa turned around and gave up a hearty fist pump in midair. Yet another fist pump was seen just two days later as she hung up the phone after accepting a date invitation.

*C*assie and Treasa kept quite busy during the day leading up to her date. Treasa accompanied Cassie to a variety of stores.

"We need to find you the perfect outfit," Cassie said as she grabbed the keys and motioned for the young girl to follow. Treasa honestly wasn't sure who was more excited with the prospect of the evening, but she got swept away in the emotion of it all as well.

The two bought everything from shoes to hair bows, and before they knew it, Treasa had a brand-new outfit from top to bottom—literally! It had only been a few weeks since the two had discovered that they were family, but Cassie was doing her best to make up for lost time. Though she'd had no control over the events that had kept them from knowing one another for all of those years, Cassie felt a sense of obligation, residing closely to guilt about how Treasa too had been raised as an orphan. She had lived with the pain of abandonment for many years as a child as well, and wished that she could have spared Treasa from ever having to learn that feeling.

Cassie thought of the day when she met this teenage girl in that orphanage, and of the connection she had immediately had with her. Then she realized something that she really hadn't thought of before now—that Treasa might have felt that connection too. Otherwise, why did she end up in Cassie's driveway when she left the orphanage?

Suddenly Cassie began to feel that maybe there was a touch of fate involved in the uniting of the two of them. She really didn't care how or why, though. Cassie was just glad that she had Treasa in her life now.

Treasa came bounding down the stairs from the loft. She had been far too excited about her upcoming date over the last few days to worry about such things as moving her personal belongings into the new room that Cassie had built just for her. There would be plenty of time for that. After all, she wasn't planning on going anywhere, at least not for a while.

Cassie motioned for her to halt and then insisted that her niece show a slight bit of self-control by allowing Cassie to open the door when Drew came knocking for their date.

He looked so cute standing there with a single white rose in hand when Cassie first opened the door; she almost began to laugh but thought better of it before anyone could notice. Treasa grabbed a light jacket, and off they went.

Cassie knew better than to wait up, but she really didn't think she'd be able to sleep until the kids returned. Though Cassie dozed intermittently while she waited, Treasa didn't seem too surprised when she found Cassie lying on the couch, snuggling her favorite fuzzy blanket, in front of a cozy fire, with the remains of a glass of Zinfandel resting nearby on a table.

Drew had already offered his "good night," and Cassie sat upright, pulled the blanket in around her neck, and tapped the seat next to her. The girls sat and talked until the sun came up, at which time Cassie proceeded into the kitchen to make coffee. There would be time to rest later, but for now she wanted to paint. She was just so filled with emotion over the smile on Treasa's face, which seemed to be reflecting the sun. Cassie felt inspiration unlike anything she had felt in years.

Over the next couple of years, Cassie watched her niece grow into such a beautiful young woman. Her heart felt full whenever she witnessed Treasa and Drew, arm in arm. It reminded her of when she too had felt a warm embrace from the man who unquestionably had belonged by her side in life. It now seemed like decades since she had felt that way about anyone, and it was absolutely heartwarming to see that emotion in the eyes of Treasa, the one person who had filled the emptiness that had existed in Cassie's heart for the last several years.

Cassie had been brought into this relationship too, as they included her in so many of their activities. She feared that they were pity invitations and at times would decline merely on principle.

But one day, Drew and Treasa came back early from what had started out as a typical date. But as the couple approached her, Cassie noticed that they were adorning even bigger smiles than normal. This time they motioned for her to sit down next to them on the couch.

Drew took a few minutes to light a fire while Cassie finished drying her dishpan hands and then joined them in the adjacent room, during which time Treasa grabbed three champagne flutes from the cabinet.

Cassie was all but giddy; she had begun to develop a theory about what was happening. She was certain there was about to be a major change in their lives once more—this time in a very good way. But she took her seat and sat patiently while the two kids told her the news. Treasa and Drew shared a wink and a smile as the glasses were filled and everyone took their respective seats near the fire.

"Aunt Cassie, you know how much you mean to me, right?" Treasa began.

But before Cassie could even respond, Drew piped in with, "And how much you have grown to mean to me."

Feeling sure that she had indeed been on the right track, Cassie simply replied with a smile of love and acceptance, followed by a quick wink to Treasa as well.

Overcome with excitement and unbounding joy, Treasa busted in, reaching out her left hand and saying, "Look, Aunt Cassie!" as she held one finger prominently above the rest, revealing a brightly shining diamond ring.

Drew then busted in with a serious demeanor and said, "But it's not official yet. It will not be until we have your blessing. Treasa and I both feel very strongly about that fact."

Cassie became completely overcome with emotion, and the two wondered if they had approached this in the right manner. They told her that it was not their intention to make her cry.

She grabbed the corner of the fuzzy blanket that seemed to reside permanently in its little corner of the couch and began dabbing at her eyes. "Oh, dear, sweet children," she began. "You both have become such blessings in my life over the years. I am truly blessed that you have been brought into my days. But I knew that the time would come when you would have to leave and make your way without me in this big, beautiful world. Please don't give me a second thought as I love you both so very much and realize that you deserve happiness—the same happiness I once shared with the man of my dreams."

Now feeling slightly embarrassed that they hadn't made their desires clear from the start, Drew resumed his explanation. "First off, I would be honored if you would allow me to call you Aunt Cassie as well."

With pride, she replied with an accepting nod.

"In that case, Aunt Cassie," he continued, "I want you to realize something right from the start. I have no intention of removing this cherished beauty from your daily life. Before even asking her to be my wife, I put an offer down on a piece of land to build us a house."

Again, Cassie was uncertain of exactly where he was going with this, but she felt the need to allow him to proceed.

Drew walked to the front door, opened it, and motioned for her to join him there. "Do you see that wooded lot down the street?" he asked. "That is the property that I have decided to purchase, the place I intend to build our home—if you will have us as neighbors, that is."

Her tears once more flowed freely as Cassie realized her biggest fears had now been addressed and overcome. She had never wanted Treasa to feel that she needed to stay with her forever, but Cassie also had known the intense pain that comes with coping with loneliness. Her fears were now replaced by answered dreams.

The months ahead were filled with wedding plans. Dawn was excited to be included in the planning process, and the three women spent several mornings discussing wedding options over coffee.

While Drew had come from a very large family, Treasa wanted to make the day an intimate affair, much like what she had heard in the stories that Cassie had shared over the years, when they discussed the time when her love had been young and new all those years ago.

All the while these discussions were taking place, the women could hear the pounding of hammers from down the street as Drew spent every spare moment creating a home for himself and his intended bride.

Drew's relationship with his family had not been one of much closeness, and while he and Treasa both referred to Cassie as Aunt Cassie, they both looked to her as more of a mother figure. Cassie reckoned that his estrangement from his own family was part of the reason why he encouraged Treasa in her desire to keep their special day small and simple.

Cassie had been quite aware of their admiration and respect for her, and she was willing to accept the responsibilities that it included. She had already shown this willingness in many ways, ever since the day she moved Treasa into her home several years ago, but she reaffirmed it when she offered to pay forward the favor that her mother figure had given her and Thad almost a quarter of a century ago.

Treasa recalled hearing the stories that Cassie had told of that magical weekend when her love was new. While she felt that it was undoubtedly an awesome experience, she did not want Cassie to go to that much trouble. Cassie assured her that it would be her pleasure, but she eventually, but rather reluctantly, backed down as Treasa insisted that her dreams were simple.

The day had finally arrived. Cassie stood at the base of the wooden staircase that wrapped around her fireplace and led to the loft hanging above. As she looked adoringly at the beautiful woman standing at its crest all dressed in white, Cassie could only see the teenage girl who had captured her heart all those years ago, when she'd first walked into the art room of the orphanage.

Dawn began playing "Canon in D" on Cassie's beautiful baby grand piano, which had done little more than attract cobwebs and dust for much of its existence, ever since Cassie had decided to cover up the keyboard and pick up a paintbrush.

Treasa, carefully and with much precision, followed the stairway down to meet the people who had become so important to her. Cassie reached out a hand to assist the bride in her last few steps and then continued the last few feet with her, to the outreaching hand of her new and forever love. As the couple faced the glistening fireplace, vows and rings were exchanged in a very traditional manner. It wasn't exactly what Cassie had hoped for, but this was Treasa's day, and it was exactly what her niece had envisioned.

Cassie had at least convinced the couple to allow her to send them on a honeymoon. Drew had been dealing with a heavy and unpredicted workload, because he had put a few projects to the side in order to finish their home in time for the wedding, so he was only able to take a few days off. The couple had talked of visiting Niagara Falls, and that was where Cassie sent them.

Drew and Treasa had been clear on one other fact about the honeymoon as well. They wanted spontaneity and the fun that comes with letting events unfold for themselves. Cassie told them that she understood, and she sneakily placed a preloaded cash card into Treasa's purse, which allowed them the ability to do most anything they desired along the way. Cassie knew that the newlyweds could have managed all right without her financial support, but she really felt the need to do something since they hadn't allowed her to give them an extravagant wedding.

Cassie spent the following days with paintbrush in hand and very little else. She had forgotten just how lonely it felt to live alone. Treasa had added so much joy to her daily life, as well as the security of knowing that she would always have love in her life—something that comes from having true family.

Looking around at the paint-covered canvases sitting along the wall of the loft, the very same wall that so many other paintings had vacated to make room for a bed for Treasa on the day that she moved in, Cassie realized that life is so unpredictable—and she now noticed and finally accepted that as a good thing.

*C*assie looked at a mirror that had been hanging in the corner since the day she'd left the home she'd shared with Thad all those years ago. Cassie wasn't sure if she had even bothered to look into that mirror since that night she'd lost Thad, as she'd been preparing for work. She remembered feeling as though she would never breathe again, much less smile.

But now, without her even realizing which day it had happened, her life had changed yet again, and that part of her heart had stopped aching—for the most part. Instead, when she took the time to stop and think about her days with Thad, she didn't think of that last one. No, she now focused on the good ones—the everyday ones. She recalled the days of barbecues and beers with Tammy and Steve, and the fun times they'd shared.

Suddenly something urged her to switch her focus to the calendar that hung on the wall nearby. She had used this calendar for work purposes, marking off objectives and goals in order to meet exhibit obligations. This time she did not look at the work notes. Instead she just looked at the date, and a realization came upon her. It was something that she had not even thought about for several years: today was her wedding anniversary. Her mind wandered back to her wedding day, and she wondered why the wonderful people she'd spent it with had so suddenly occupied her mind for what seemed like no reason at all.

Cassie rinsed her brushes, removed her apron, and proceeded down the steps to the closet she had avoided since the day she had moved to the cabin. As she searched through boxes of memories, Cassie found a photo album that, other than being a bit dusty, appeared to be brand new. Cassie had not looked at this album since the day the movers had placed it into the box as they packed her belongings shortly after Thad's accident, in preparation for the move.

Then something startled her. One of the pictures contained an object in the background: a heart-shaped picture frame that had contained a photo Tammy had taken when Thad had placed the ring on Cassie's finger that day on the trolley in Memphis. It was a gift that Thad had given to her as she'd sat across from him at the dinner table on their first anniversary.

After scouring through the remaining boxes in the closet, it saddened her to see that this picture frame and photo were nowhere to be found. Had it been left behind, tucked somewhere on a shelf and overlooked by the movers, strangers she had allowed to take on such important tasks as packing her most valued possessions? It should have been her responsibility to do this. She would have made sure that the picture had been in the truck when they left. But now that she was finally prepared to hold a tangible reminder of her memories with Thad, it was no longer an option for her.

She sat for a while longer, rummaging through boxes looking for the heart-shaped frame, but she finally resigned herself to the fact that it no longer existed in her world. So she decided to spend a little time taking a trip down a road she didn't often travel anymore—memory lane! She took her time, taking in the full effect of every single memory that had attached itself to each of the photos in the album. It had been such a long time since she had really stopped to relive the times she had shared with Thad, let alone with Tammy and Steve. She smiled all the while, realizing once more how far she had come since the day she had left the orphanage a lifetime ago.

She then revisited the time when she had been rescued by her knight in shining armor as he pulled that big rig off onto the shoulder. Cassie recalled how she had felt the panic of being stranded, until a sense of peace had come upon her as she'd taken that first glimpse at his adorable face.

Now for the first time in a long time—maybe for the first time since she had answered that phone call at work the day of Thad's death—she thought back to that life and explored where she might be now had Thad's accident not happened.

She realized that she was no longer the woman who had answered that 9-1-1 call. That woman no longer existed. The other thing she realized was that, now, there wasn't any guilt attached to that observation.

At one time, she'd felt that it was a great disservice to his memory for her to be happy and find a new way in life. But she had grown to realize that, during their years together, he had only wanted her happiness. She should have no reason to think that he would feel otherwise in death.

Because he had loved her so much all those years ago, she had been able to find a new life now. She had begun living her life again not in spite of him, but because of him.

It was obvious to her that he'd had a major impact on the person she had become, even since his death. She had to admit that her past was an important part of the woman that she had become—the very same woman who had looked back at her in the mirror a few hours before.

Just then the phone rang. She was surprised to hear the voice on the other end. It was Blu. "Cassie, how are you?" he began.

She got the customary "I'm fine" out, but little more, before he cut her off with excitement.

"I have a fantastic offer for you, one that I hope you will give serious consideration," he said, barely catching his breath. "There is a prominent family in France who is looking for an artist to come to their villas and do some freelance work. The couple seems to be very eccentric, and they are in hopes that by having work done this way, they will maintain consistency throughout. I know that in addition to wall hangings in several rooms, there are also ideas for a few murals as well. They will pay all accommodations in addition to a healthy stipend. The family anticipates that it will take the better part of a year to fulfill the obligations outlined in the job. I immediately thought of you and wanted to see if you had the flexibility and desire to take on such a task."

"I will have to take a little time to think about this Blu," Cassie said. "I think I should discuss this with Treasa and Drew. I suppose even Dawn needs to be consulted. When do they need my decision?"

"The sooner the better," was all he said.

"Then I will call you early next week, once the kids have returned from their honeymoon," she said just before she returned the telephone to its cradle.

Cassie had no intention of interrupting the young couple on their trip, but her excitement had taken her over too much to just sit and keep it contained. So she invited Dawn over for coffee and a chat.

The two sat for the better part of the afternoon and well into the evening. "I think I need something a bit stronger than coffee, Cassie. Do you have any of my favorite wine chilled by chance?" Dawn asked, also getting caught up in the emotion of the prospect for Cassie.

Cassie headed to the kitchen, where she retired their coffee cups to the sink. She then returned to the living room with two of her best crystal wine goblets and a bottle of champagne leftover from her niece's wedding just days before. "I think this calls for a special treat. I am going to do it as long as Treasa and Drew don't object," Cassie said as she took her place next to Dawn once again.

"You know that you have my complete support, and I assure you that the kids will agree, just in case you have to give your answer before you get a chance to talk with them. You have to realize that it is your life to live, and they will say that this is your decision to make. I have every reason to believe that they will support you in whatever you choose to do in life. You've always thought things through before, and I have every reason to believe that even in this short amount of time, you already have put more thought into this than most do in a month of Sundays," her long-winded friend said between sips.

Cassie smiled. "Thanks, Dawn. I knew that I could count on you. But there is still so much to figure out. I just don't want Treasa to think that I am leaving her behind. What if she needs me?" She had in fact already given the prospect full consideration, analyzing it from all angles.

"Cassie, I actually think it might be good for all of you. The kids need to learn how to build a life together, and this would be the perfect time for them to start," Dawn wisely replied.

Days later, Treasa and Drew returned, and Cassie informed them of her offer over a nice dinner, drinks, and picture sharing. The kids were thrilled for her, much like Dawn had said they would be—and Cassie had been sure they would be as well.

"Aunt Cassie, you have put so much of your life on hold for me over the past few years, and I know that it has not always been easy for you, even though you never let it show," Treasa said.

Cassie realized that her niece had become a grown woman and was capable of entering the next phase of her life. In fact, she realized that Dawn was right. She needed to take this offer as much for Treasa and Drew as she needed it for herself.

The next morning, Cassie called Blu and accepted the offer. Three weeks later she was on a plane, crossing the ocean to experience life in a different land, one she had never considered herself visiting before.

he LeBaux family was quite generous in their arrangements. As a limousine picked her and several bags up, heading to the airport, Cassie began to realize that she was entering a completely different lifestyle than what she'd become accustomed to. She enjoyed first-class accommodations all the way, something she had never encountered before, with the exception of that memorable weekend in Memphis all those years ago.

When she arrived at the villas, Cassie felt that she was seeing paradise firsthand. The splendor she had seen in her other trips paled in comparison. It was if she had been producing blank canvases up to this point, since she could have never imagined, much less captured, the beauty that lay before her now.

As she settled into one of the villas, she was overcome with awe. She looked out one window and saw water as far as the eye could see. The hue was unlike any she had ever seen. In a way, it reminded her of the color of Thad's eyes. The water was so blue and soothing that just to see it would put the most uptight person at ease. Now that her memory of those beautiful blue eyes had all but disappeared in her mind, it was a beauty that she couldn't compare to anything. She was so in love with the sight that it captured her mind for several hours. Cassie decided to step out the French doors leading from her immaculate living quarters onto the veranda for a better view.

As she felt the warm, but not hot, temperatures softly caressing her face, she just sat and intently watched the still waters. It was at this moment that she realized she had finally found paradise.

She turned around and walked to the back rooms to explore her home—at least her home for the next several months. As she approached the back of her villa, Cassie spotted yet another set of doors leading to more explorations. While the mountains didn't appear to be as high as what she had seen in her travels out West, they were every bit as majestic.

As she looked a little farther into the distance, she caught a glimpse of a structure so large that her own nations capitol building would have gotten lost within the grounds and all they hosted. It was days before she realized this structure was her reason for being there. Cassie understood why they had asked her to plan for such a lengthy stay and why her trip had been so elaborate up to this point. This was no small job, and the family who had hired her knew it.

But she never doubted her abilities to complete the task. Blu had seen to that, always building her up, it seemed. While their relationship had ended abruptly, he always had faith in her talents as well as the driving force behind them.

"As stated in the contract we sent to you, we will furnish all the supplies you could possibly need to complete the project," her new employer began. "Tomorrow we will head out and begin lining up everything you could possibly need or want. For now, just enjoy the scenery and begin getting acclimated."

"Thank you so much for this opportunity, Mr. LeBeaux. I sure hope I can live up to your expectations," Cassie replied.

"I have little doubt of that. You came very highly recommended," he said.

"I think that Blu may exaggerate just a bit about my potential, but I will give this my best shot," she said, almost apologetically.

"Oh, trust me on this, we did not hire you on his recommendation alone, Cassie." With that, he quickly turned and made his exit.

Cassie would have loved to ask about any other recommendations on her behalf, but she recognized in his eager exit that this might be a subject she would be wise to dismiss—at least for now.

The next day was filled with shopping trips to obtain everything she needed. A small villa next to hers had been made up as a suitable studio so that she could work any time inspiration hit, but it was not in her quarters, so she could also walk away when she needed the escape.

Though she was quite worn out, between all of the shopping and the jet lag, Cassie could hardly resist the urge to get started on her paintings. She could think of nothing more inspirational than the vision she had before her and couldn't wait to dip her paintbrush into the wide array of colors on the pallet.

Even though this was a temporary situation, Cassie still had to reflect back and realize that she did not even resemble the woman who had been married to that wonderful man years ago, let alone the small child who had felt abandoned in that cold, dank orphanage.

On occasion, Mr. LeBeaux would round up his crew and ask Cassie to join them for a relaxing sail across the still waters. Cassie, feeling so overwhelmed by her new lifestyle, almost forgot her fear of water and excitedly said yes to his offer. No sooner had her foot reached the edge of the dock, however, when her tremendous fear of the waters came rushing back.

But these waters were different. The mesmerizing stillness, combined with the beautiful bluish hue, almost hypnotized her. While she had felt a bit of hesitation as she took that first step onto Mr. LeBeaux's sailboat, Cassie was more than eager to rejoin them on future sails. After all, he had a highly trained crew, and as soon as she'd made this observation, she was able to leave her fears dockside.

Cassie knew that if she spent much more time in this beautiful land, her heart would never want to return from whence it had come. This created an irrational driving force in her—homesickness plus the longing to be in the arms of her family, a family she had lived for so many years not knowing. She yearned for a quick completion of the project.

An occasional call or text from either Dawn or Treasa would indicate that all was well back home. But that was very little consolation for her. She was surrounded by so much beauty, but all she could think about now was sitting with her warm, fuzzy blanket next to a cozy fire, her hands wrapped around a steaming-hot cup of coffee.

After what seemed to her as a rather long ten months, she completely fulfilled her obligation. With plane ticket in hand, she once more climbed into an airport limousine waiting to return her to a place she had grown to miss so much. While she had been so full of excitement and intrigue about what had lay ahead when she had climbed into that similar vehicle months ago, nothing could compare to the happiness she felt, now that she was returning to her home—and her family.

It was a tearful departure, when she left for home. Cassie had been overwhelmed by the reception and hospitality she had received from the moment that chauffeur had met her at baggage claim when her plane had first landed on foreign soil. But they weren't her family, and they had been little substitute, though she was quite certain that they had tried.

*N*othing could compare to the sight Cassie saw as she reached baggage claim at the end of her return flight. As she approached the carousel, she spotted Dawn, Drew and Treasa standing before her in the distance. Cassie was so excited at the sight of the three people she'd grown to love more than life itself that she overlooked the obvious.

Though she didn't notice it right away, Cassie suddenly realized that Treasa and Drew were just a few months away from bringing a new addition into the family. Tears of joy filled her eyes as she embraced her niece. Drew grabbed Cassie's arm and swung her around to get a bit of that welcoming response as well.

"Aunt Cassie, we have missed you so much," Drew said.

"I have so much to tell you, Aunt Cassie," Treasa interrupted. "I don't even know where to begin."

Cassie felt yet another jolt. Dawn had not been too far behind in her welcoming grip. "You have no idea how much we have all missed you, and I've been biting my tongue for too long—at your niece and nephew's request, you realize," her friend told her amid the tears that had begun welling up in the corners of her eyes.

Cassie was just thankful to be back in the loving arms of her family.

Though the ride back home was not nearly as extravagant as the lifestyle her host family had tried to familiarize her with during the many months prior, Cassie felt that the moments she was experiencing right now had little comparison. She was elated to be back where she knew she belonged.

She wondered if she had ever felt as much love and emotion as she did now, but then she realized that it was much like she had felt when Thad had showered her with his love and affection back when their love had been new. She had known the sense of belonging then as well, though she had spent several years now trying to forget, in an effort to ease the intense pain.

She breathed a sigh of relief as she stepped into her front room and saw that those she had grown to appreciate as family had taken good care of her home in her absence. She was stunned by the beautiful bouquet that adorned the mantle, but she became even more stunned to find out that no one was taking responsibility for its presence. There was no card attached, but it was filled with an assortment of tulips, calla lilies, roses, and carnations—her very favorite flowers. This was no mistake. Someone who had known her quite well had been responsible for their arrival and she intended to find out who.

While she had no idea where to begin on her pathway to discovery, she decided to begin with a call to Blu. He was the logical choice. After all, he would have known of her exact itinerary. He replied to her inquiry by saying, "No, Cassie. I did not have the flowers delivered, but maybe I should have. You certainly earned them. I did want to call you when you got settled to let you know that the LeBeaux family was more than pleased with your work. Also, they have assured me that the final payment will be transferred into your account by the end of the business day today, if it is not there already."

Later that day, she was stunned when she received confirmation of the final payment as it was posted to her bank account. It was far more than the agreed-upon amount, and Cassie soon realized that she could afford a much higher lifestyle.

She debated at first whether to sell her cabin and move into something a bit more conducive to the conditions she had learned to live under during her adventure. But she soon realized that she needed to stay where her heart knew contentment and peace. Cassie decided that her happiness resided between the modest walls she had found so pleasing when she had made the leap and decided to leave the only other place she had ever called home in her adult life.

For a brief period of time, she was distracted from her investigation. But that didn't last long, and she was back to it, trying to find out who her secret admirer had been. Her next thought was of the family she had gotten to know recently, while she had been under their employ. But this seemed like more of a romantic gesture than compensation, so it was even more impractical than her suspicion that they had been ordered by Blu.

At one point during her mission, she even considered that these flowers could have been a gift from Roger. Cassie became a bit saddened when she realized that it had been a couple of years since she had seen him, and she wondered if he was still living in the little house behind hers in the old neighborhood. She then began wondering if he was okay.

He picked up the phone on the first ring, as though Roger had been sitting by the phone, waiting for her call. They chatted for a while about life and the changes and challenges they'd faced since the last time they'd spoken. Cassie was happy to know that he was still living in the same house and now had someone special in his life. She hung up the phone, feeling that she might never see him again. Life had just changed so much for her, and they had grown apart. While it saddened her to think about it, Cassie had to face reality.

Weeks later, the flowers had wilted, and so had her search. She spent her summer days taking long walks and just exploring once more the beauty that her homeland had to offer.

But Cassie was brought back to reality on one hot July morning with the unexpected ringing of the phone. After being away for so long, Cassie had decided to just stay close by as Treasa and Drew awaited the arrival of the newest family member. Cassie had gotten accustomed to a silent telephone. No one in her life seemed to call anymore. With everyone she spoke to in her daily routine within walking distance, they had all just learned to show up unannounced.

She was stunned to hear Drew's voice on the line. He would have been the last one she would have expected to be hearing from on this particular day. "Aunt Cassie, I am at the hospital with Treasa. Everything is fine with her, but I think you should come as soon as you can."

She hardly finished getting dressed, let alone tying her shoes, before sprinting to her car. A quick phone call to Dawn as she approached the end of the lane gave her the peace of knowing that her friend would be by her side as she sat and waited for what she was certain was the birth of her great-nephew.

When she arrived, Drew was standing near the entrance to the waiting room as though there to escort Cassie to her chair. He caught her by the elbow as she made her entrance to the room. He wanted to inform her of the day's events. "Aunt Cassie," Drew began. "The doctors assure me that even though he is coming a bit early, our baby should be completely fine."

Cassie searched Drew's eyes for a sign of what he was about to say but found nothing there, so she allowed him to continue. "Treasa was going about her daily chores when I heard her answer the phone. Apparently it was

Mrs. Lavour's nurse. She was calling to inform Treasa that the old woman had passed away a few days ago. She seemed to be indifferent about it at first, but they think that the anxiety may have triggered premature labor."

Cassie interrupted, "I need to see my niece right this instant." Drew had never seen this side of her before. She had always been so calm and laid back. It struck him completely by surprise. But he led the way, and the two entered the labor room together.

Treasa was still in the early stages of labor, but the doctor felt that it would be best to just let nature run its course this time. After spending a few minutes with her, Cassie realized that Treasa was sad about her adoptive grandmother. She had never gotten to know the older woman, and she had all the family she needed now—especially since she was about to become a mom. But it was still the end of a life, and she felt the loss.

"I am going to join Dawn out in the waiting room now, guys," Cassie told the young couple. "Treasa, I am so very proud of you and can't wait to meet our newest addition to the family." She headed toward the large double doors leading from the birthing room.

It turned into a long night, but everyone remained at the hospital, awaiting news. At 5:45 a.m. on that Sunday morning in July, the six-pound, fifteen-ounce bundle of joy, Carlton Sperling, joined the world. He was perfect in every way and was adored from the instant they first spotted his rosy little cheeks.

Until that moment, Cassie had never experienced such joy. She had never really thought much about it, but this was the first time she had ever held a newborn baby. She had been near them back in her younger days, in the orphanage. But she had never spent much time around the babies there and had really never given newborns much consideration, since it hadn't been likely that she and Thad would ever have children. Then Cassie considered that she'd had a baby sister who had been separated from her when they were both very young. This moment with Carlton was indeed special.

After a two-day stay at the community hospital, Treasa and Drew brought their son home. Though Cassie was a bit apprehensive at first, she enjoyed spending time holding and playing with her great-nephew. She even wondered if the new parents would allow her to babysit, since she was so inexperienced and nervous. But once Treasa and Drew were ready to spend a little adult time together, Aunt Cassie was the first sitter on the list—followed closely by Aunt Dawn.

Cassie was so thankful that she had stayed close by instead of buying a new home when the opportunity had arisen months before. She couldn't imagine living away from Treasa and her family. Even across town would have felt so far away from her now, and she had grown to appreciate having such a handy man across the street—just in case something would go wrong around the house.

*I*t was a hot Tuesday in late July when Cassie looked out the window and noticed the large black sedan turning into her driveway. She wondered what that could be about, once she realized that it was not there merely to turn around.

A medium-built gentleman, dressed to the nines, got out of the car with briefcase in hand and made his approach toward her front door. Cassie wasn't accustomed to having strangers just stopping by.

The man rang the doorbell, and Cassie reluctantly opened the door, with the chain firmly in place. "I am Mr. Patrick Slezinger from the law offices of Slezinger and Logan. I am here to speak to Mrs. Malone and Mrs. Sperling. Are you by chance one of these two ladies?"

"I am Mrs. Malone. Mrs. Sperling is my niece," began a somewhat timid Cassie. She couldn't imagine what this lawyer could possibly want with the two of them. "Give me just a minute, and I will call Treasa and see if she is available to come down. Could you wait here for just a bit?" She turned to walk back inside, closing the front door.

She quickly called Treasa. "Could you come down as soon as possible and bring Drew along if he's home?" Cassie asked in an excited tone.

Curiosity had certainly gotten the best of her, but she decided to wait to allow the man to enter her home as she watched Treasa and Drew approach from their house just down the street. Cassie removed the chain and stepped outside. Moments later, Dawn's car pulled up, with Treasa and Drew walking right behind. Hearing the excitement in her aunt's voice, Treasa had called Dawn before heading across the street.

"Carlton is asleep. I brought our monitor, but one of us will need to run down and check on him momentarily," Treasa said just before her foot approached the top step leading to the cabin's front door.

The five adults entered Cassie's home and were seated around the cozy area surrounding the empty fireplace. Mr. Slezinger motioned, asking permission, as he placed his briefcase on the coffee table in front of him. Cassie offered an approving nod, and he continued to make his business known to them.

"As I stated when I first arrived here, I am Patrick Slezinger, and I am with the law offices of Slezinger and Logan. We represent the estate of the late Mrs. Lavour. Do you ladies happen to know of this woman?" questioned the guest.

"Yes, we have met her," Cassie said. "What would her estate attorney need with us, though? We hardly knew her."

"Mrs. Lavour summoned me to her home several months ago when she realized that her health was rapidly declining. Our firm has represented her family for generations, and she stated that she had a few things to make right before she left this world. She informed me that she'd had a rather good life, but one thing was missing above all else. Mrs. Lavour had always regretted that she had allowed her husband to force upon her some of the bad choices he had made," the attorney said. "She spoke of how she had always missed the little girl whom they had raised as their own in years past, and how excited she'd been to meet the girl's daughter as a young woman. She wished that she could have been an active grandmother to the girl. But by the time they met, the woman's health just no longer allowed this. She was happy to know that her granddaughter had made contact with the one true family member she had, an aunt. In fact, for a brief period of time, she seemed to be getting stronger after this aunt had brought the girl to the woman on that day when they all finally met."

Tears began to fill Cassie's and Treasa's eyes; they regretted that they had not made more attempts to visit her since that day.

As he pulled a folder from within his briefcase, he continued, "You may not have been aware of this, but Mrs. Lavour's family had left her with considerable assets. Her husband had insisted that they live the moderate lifestyle he had grown accustomed to since childhood. He had been a very proud man and had refused to support her with the influence of her family's money. He was going to be the breadwinner, and that was all there was to it. Truth is, I met him on occasion over the years. Mr. Lavour was what I would consider to be somewhat of a tyrant."

Cassie and Treasa glanced at one another curiously. Would the old woman whom they had met only the one time actually consider leaving them something upon her death? What about the nurse who had taken care of her all those years—wasn't she entitled to that? Cassie began asking the attorney these very same questions, as she was certain the thoughts were in Treasa's head as well.

"I assure you, Mrs. Lavour did compensate her assistant in an appropriate manner. But she felt that you
two were family, something she had lived without for
many years. She was adamant about leaving you both
equal shares of the bulk of her rather sizable estate. She
stated that, after that day when you two visited, she began
watching you both from afar and kept informed of your
comings and goings. The woman was aware, at the time
of her death, that Treasa had married and even expecting a boy. There has also been a trust fund set up for
this young child that will allow him access to great wealth
once he is a grown man."

These words were almost more than Treasa and
Cassie could comprehend. Drew stepped in and said that
their son had, in fact, entered the world just weeks before. The lawyer nodded; he'd had suspicions, based on
the thinner-than-expected Treasa who sat before him.

Mr. Slezinger wrapped up his visit by saying, "Mrs.
Lavour told me that she had two regrets during her lifetime and intended to make things as right as she could
while there was still time. The first regret was in allowing her husband enough control to keep her from
adopting both girls from the orphanage, rather than
just Angie. And the second that she again allowed him to
control a situation that ultimately broke two hearts—the
day he asked the girl she had known as her only child
to leave their home, never to return. Mrs. Lavour never

recovered from either of those events, and she stated if she had not been committed to her marriage, she would have left him that day."

The man left after telling them that the necessary papers were being drawn up and that he would be in touch once everything was finalized. Cassie and Treasa looked at each other, still with tears in their eyes. They'd had no idea they had meant that much to Mrs. Lavour.

While Drew had a decent job, it was clear that this new development would have major implications for all concerned. Cassie, having already earned a substantial amount to support her current lifestyle, informed Dawn that she wanted to make sure that she was taken care of as well. Dawn had lived a modest life, and while she never made it clear in so many words, Cassie had noticed that her friend was struggling financially.

No decisions were made at that point. Cassie and Treasa had a lot to talk about, and they both realized that. But the day had already been far too overwhelming for everyone concerned, so they decided that they all needed to take a little time to think—to process all of this information.

*D*ays turned into weeks and weeks into months. The papers were now finalized, baby Carlton was old enough to travel, and the five of them decided to take a vacation to see parts unknown.

Cassie, Dawn, Drew, and Treasa packed bags and began an adventure, with Carlton in tow, unlike anything they had ever experienced before. They found themselves starting stateside. Cassie had told them so much of her months in France that they had decided to explore a little outside of the country as well.

They didn't return home until they had spent two weeks in Europe, ending the trip by visiting the LeBeaux family and even skiing down the Swiss Alps.

After two months of fun and games, they all found it necessary to return home and try to figure out what their futures were going to hold. Cassie decided that she needed to return to her artwork. She had grown to realize that she was much happier with a paintbrush in her hand, so at least that much of her course was set, it seemed.

Once her bags were unpacked, Cassie began thinking about the next phase of her life. She had heard that Blu was considering shutting down the gallery and decided to find out more about his reasons. Now that they all had the ability to make significant life changes, there were many possibilities to consider.

"Good morning, dear," was the response she heard when Blu answered the phone. He seemed genuinely thrilled to be getting this call from her. She wondered if he had been aware of her new windfall—or was he just happy to hear the voice of his dear old friend? Cassie didn't care. The truth was that she was just as happy to hear his voice.

She had missed the friendship they had once shared and wanted to make sure that he was okay. "I've heard that you are considering shutting down the gallery. Is that true, Blu?" asked Cassie in a sullen tone. While she no longer needed his assistance, even if she intended to continue her career, she had realized how big of a part of his life this gallery had been, and she wanted to make sure that he was making this decision based on the right factors.

"Is this decision based on financial matters?" Cassie asked.

"Sweet Cassie, this is really none of your concern. You no longer need me or the gallery. I will make sure that all of my contacts in the art world are aware of your abilities if they don't already know. However, you have made quite a name for yourself, especially after the contract work you did in France. You do realize that you are now world renowned in the art world, don't you?" Blu said proudly.

Cassie sat in silence, unsure of how to reply to his remark.

Cassie continued by telling him that she was considering jumping the fence to his side of the business. "Would you consider a silent partner?" she asked, once she realized that her theory that he was having financial woes might have been correct.

After listening to his conflicted words and vocal inflection, she decided that a trip to the city was warranted. This was not a conversation that she wanted to continue over the phone. She ended the call by telling him, "I would love to meet you for lunch soon and discuss this further."

"I would like to see you again, dear. It has been such a long time," he agreed, and a tentative date was made.

Meanwhile, Cassie and Treasa decided to do a little online investigating about the family who'd raised Angie. The two women had realized long ago that this may be their only chance of finding out more about Treasa's birth mother. In no time at all, they found someone who had been related to Angie's adopted family, and correspondence began.

After several weeks of phone calls and online chats, Cassie and Treasa decided to bundle up Carlton and take him on another plane ride. The snow was just beginning to fall as Drew pulled up to the departure lane to drop them off for their flight. They were quite relieved at the prospect of being down south when the first real snowfall of the season hit the Midwest.

It wasn't going to be a long flight, like they had encountered during their recent trip to the Swiss Alps, and Cassie knew that Treasa was quite relieved. The airline attendants had been very helpful with the baby during that flight, but the experience had nevertheless been somewhat trying on the new mom. Carlton had been such a small infant when they'd taken their extended vacation, but now he was feeling the urge to move around more, adding even a bit more of a challenge to the plane ride.

When they arrived at their destination, they were met by an excited woman, Louise, who insisted they refer to her as "cousin," since she had been so close to Treasa's mom many years ago.

Louise hadn't known about Cassie and didn't really think that Angie had ever really been aware of her existence either. While it saddened her a bit to think that her sister had never been told, Cassie understood and decided to take comfort in the fact that Angie surely would have tried to find her if she had known.

Louise then told Treasa that she was sorry about her mom's tragic death, and while her side of the family had heard rumors of a child born out of wedlock, the Lavour family had been quite secretive about the facts regarding the whereabouts and even disappearance of Angie. That too saddened Cassie and Treasa, to think that she could have felt so loved and yet been discarded so easily.

No one knew who could have been Treasa's father, and it was quite obvious at this point that they never would know.

But the three women were elated to have connected with one another, and it was surprising to Louise how much Cassie and Treasa reminded her of Angie, the cousin she gotten to know so well, and then lost, when she had been a young girl.

Cassie and Treasa had been uncomfortable about the invitation to stay at Louise's home when she had first offered, but within minutes of spending time with her, their reservations had been put aside. Within hours, the three of them were the best of friends, acting as though they had known one another forever.

Recalling how Mrs. Lavour had said they were so much like Angie, Cassie and Treasa were not too surprised by the familiarity they all felt. Though they were not technically blood related, they felt truly blessed to feel that their family was growing—they had found a cousin.

One day, while getting pedicures side by side in massage chairs, Louise confessed, "You know, I have always felt a little guilty about Angie's situation. It took me a long time to overcome the idea that maybe she would still be here if I hadn't up and moved away with David when I did. But now I see that it's also probable that we wouldn't have you, Treasa. Meeting you girls has made me realize that sometimes things just happen, and we have to just learn to accept the circumstances as they are set before us."

Later that evening, Cassie noticed a sadness in Louise's eyes, though it eluded Treasa, and realized that it was indeed a good thing that they had decided to make this trip. The three of them returned to Louise's quaint little home and enjoyed a few Irish coffees as Louise opened up to them.

"It's been a rough few years for me, I will admit. I am so thankful that you girls came into my life when you did. My girls are all grown now. Samantha and Alicia are away at universities up north, and Tabitha is married and expecting their first child. She and her husband moved to Texas a couple years ago. I miss them all so much," Louise revealed through tears.

She told them about how David had left when she'd begun struggling with their empty nest. It appeared that her husband of twenty-six years had found what was lacking in their marriage in the arms of another woman.

"I think you are handling your divorce very well, Louise," Cassie said.

"You know, I was very bitter at first. But once the tears dried, I realized that the best way to get even with him was to get over him. So I did just that," Louise said.

The day before the plane ride home, the three of them decided to take a short road trip to visit Universal

Studios, something both Cassie and Treasa had secretly dreamed about since childhood. They all had a blast, in spite of the cold. "It makes for shorter ride lines," Treasa said flippantly.

"I really enjoyed all of the shows," Cassie replied.

"*E.T.* was, by far, my favorite ride," Treasa said.

This was no surprise for Louise or Cassie, as Treasa had dragged them there by their elbows for the fifth time that day. Cassie was happy to see her acting like a child for a change. Life seemed to be very serious for Treasa, and that concerned her aunt very much.

After a week of hilarity and merriment, it was time for the girls to return back to their homes and the rest of the family. Dawn had been taking care of Cassie's house and looking in on Drew in Treasa's absence, but Cassie and Treasa knew that they were being missed for sure. The girls looked forward to sharing stories of their trip down south and the wonderful hospitality they had been given during their stay.

Drew awaited their arrival with bated breath. He'd encountered sleepless nights in Treasa's absence. Their son had missed his daddy every bit as much as Treasa had, and the two of them had, at times, become quite irritable as a result.

Though they'd had a wonderful time during their visit with their newfound cousin, and neither was thrilled about returning to snow-covered ground, both women were happy to be arriving back at their respective homes.

Once the luggage was unpacked and she had taken a few days to rest up from her whirlwind trip, Cassie got back in touch with Blu. She felt that she had given him plenty of time to consider her offer, and frankly she was excited to begin yet another phase in her life. Cassie was pretty sure that she could convince him to accept, but she really didn't want him to feel pressured into the decision, so she was willing to let it go if he had reservations.

The two met for lunch the following day. Cassie was a bit surprised when he countered back to her with the offer of a full-fledged partnership. The silent-partner option had been extended to him because she believed that he had merely found himself strapped for cash. But she was happy to accept his counter, and a new partnership was formed.

"What types of changes are you thinking of implementing, or are you seeing us keeping things the same as they are now?" Blu asked.

"I would like to see us focus more on highlighting undiscovered artists from the area," she replied.

"That is a fantastic idea. I was just thinking the other day about the part I played in getting your career started. I am so proud of you and all that you have accomplished with your painting career," he answered.

Remembering how much she had grown to care for him and how much it hurt them both when their relationship had ended, Cassie just smiled and planted a quick kiss upon his cheek. Although it hadn't worked out, she had feelings for him. But it just didn't feel right somehow.

She returned home and began drawing sketches of improvements to the gallery to make the business all she envisioned. Up until the moment when Blu had bounced the idea back at her, it had never crossed Cassie's mind that she would like to be an active partner in any business, let alone his art studio. Her mind wandered down paths that opened up new worlds for them. As she sketched, the studio began to grow, and she found herself actually enjoying the project.

An addition to the back of the building would offer them the opportunity to hold art classes for a wide array of talent levels, ranging from children and beginners to more advanced artists who just needed a boost of confidence. Many artists believed that this would be a good way to be discovered, and in many instances, that is exactly what happened.

In a very short time, they had created a name for themselves in the world of undiscovered but very talented artists. Every time a new artist was found and recognized for his or her talents, Blu and Cassie became as excited as new parents. They felt as though they had given birth to many new careers.

Cassie let her mind travel onto yet another path. Remembering how she had begun her career, and the advantages that had been given, she decided to figure out a way to share resources to help others. She contacted Dawn, and the two ladies spent the better part of the weeks ahead sorting through options.

As the two explored the possibilities, Dawn informed Cassie that she had a brother who could possibly help. "I know that I never spoke of him before, but I have a brother who is very good at construction. Paul used to own a construction business and was responsible for building many of the beautiful homes on the north end of town. He is retired now, but he does like to dabble in rehab projects a bit still. I bet that he would build whatever we wanted right down to our every specification."

With more excitement than she had felt in what seemed like forever, Cassie replied, "Oh my God, that would be so awesome. Let's do it!"

Paul was very happy to be included in this project and asked that they accept his generous contribution of building this structure for the cost of becoming a partner in the foundation. Within just a few short months, the Malone Memorial Artists Academy was created for young talented artists.

The purpose of this academy was to give young and upcoming artists room and board in the early days of their careers. In order to be eligible to participate in the program, all the artist had to do was to show a few characteristics: talent was most important, followed closely by drive and ambition. As long as they lived at the academy, these artists would be given moderate deadlines. Cassie felt very good about her new project, as though she were repaying a debt.

Two men had become very instrumental in her early days of painting: Thad, with his undying love and encouragement in anything she pursued, and Blu, with the many wonderful opportunities he provided when she had been just starting out.

One night in her dreams, Cassie once again heard a familiar voice in her head. It was a voice she had not heard in years, though it had been prominent in her earlier life: Thad's. It sounded just like she remembered, always quite soothing and calming to her. "I am so proud of you, baby," the voice began. "I miss you my love. Know that I always will—until I can hold you in my arms once more."

Cassie knew that this dream was just memories of him rolling forth from her heart, but it still made her feel warm and secure, something she had not felt in a very long time. She thought about the early years in her grief journey, when she'd seemed to hear his voice a lot, and remembered how it had always turned up the corners of her mouth to the sky—and this was no different.

In the months that followed, hundreds of applicants came forth, and many new artists were discovered.

The LeBeaux family had now heard about Cassie's new foundation and contacted her to offer their assistance. What started out as a simple monetary donation quickly turned into an opportunity for many of these artists, now young and old alike, to experience some of the wonderful sites that Europe had to offer.

Cassie had mostly hung up her paintbrush now, at least as far as the art-purchasing world was involved. But she was very active in offering instruction and advice to her many program participants. The studio she shared with Blu had become a great beginning venue, and the two had gained even more respect in the art community for the quality of work their academy students were producing.

Success for Cassie was bittersweet, though. She felt that Thad was still very much responsible for her inspiration. He had always been her muse. In addition, she had never overcome the urge to share good news with him. In their days together, he had always been only a phone call away, even with thousands of miles between them. She had once grown to rely on that, and she realized that, even though she now had some very good friends and family to take that call, it just wasn't the same. She still wanted Thad.

Cassie wondered how her heart could have been allowed to trust someone whom she had never met. The fact was that Larry could have been standing right next to her, and she would have never known it was him. There had just been something so comfortable about their chats, and she missed them. This made her wonder if her chat buddy was still around. It had been a long time since she had turned on her computer, but right away noticed that, lo and behold, there were recent messages from him. It was as though he had been waiting all this time for her to ask. Cassie searched deep inside herself before deciding whether or not to send him a message.

Larry accepted her chat request within minutes, and the conversation seemed to pick up right where they had left off.

Cassie had been so hurt when he'd declared love for his wife—a woman she hadn't even realized existed until that very moment. But in time, she had grown to see that, while he hadn't been completely upfront with her, Larry had never really encouraged her either. It had been her suggestion to meet—not his. And he had never asked for her heart—she had just given it to him.

Finding herself prepared, and even happy for him this time when he acknowledged love for his wife, it re-minded her of the love she had once shared with Thad. Cassie was glad that her friend had found that type of love as well. Her heart had healed from its loss—at least as much as it was going to. Realizing over time that it wasn't so much the idea of having a man in her life, it was Thad that she had been missing.

Cassie's family and friends were quick to witness the change in her demeanor and interpreted it as a result of her newfound success with the studio and academy. They knew that Thad still held a big part of her heart, and it never dawned on them to suspect that she had reconnected with Larry. She knew better than to tell them yet because they had been so concerned about her when the two had parted ways years before.

*C*assie kept quite busy, and time flew most days now. But she truly loved her life, even though there was a void that had never been filled. She just had learned how to smile through the emptiness.

Before she knew it, her great-nephew had celebrated his second birthday. It amazed her to think that so many years had passed since an eighteen-year-old Treasa had waited patiently in the driveway in front of the cabin for Cassie to come home.

Cassie remembered how reluctant she had been to bring someone into her house as she had grown rather accustomed to spending the majority of time alone, and she remembered realizing that she would have to sacrifice her art studio to give the young girl more than just a couch to sleep on, let alone a bit of privacy. It hadn't taken long to realize that the latter was in limited supply in the cabin.

Thinking back to the day when Drew and his crew had arrived to build the addition, Cassie thought about how the accommodations she had built for her newly discovered niece had actually been nicer than the room she had taken for her own. In fact, it was more like a suite. Why had she never considered moving into the space after Treasa and Drew got married?

She recruited the help of Drew and Treasa to assist with the actual moving of the furniture.

They transferred the bed and other furniture that remained in what had become the guest room (though it never really got used unless Carlton spent the night) into Cassie's old room, making herself at home in the suite out back.

Cassie figured that if the occasion ever arose again that guests needed to make themselves comfortable in her home, they would be more than welcome to use the room that had served as her bedroom for so many years.

In the midst of the move, the occasion arose for her to once more view the calendar that had hung on the studio wall. Cassie suddenly realized that it once again announced the date that she had once celebrated, but now dreaded.

Her memory went back to a special weekend spent with people that she had loved so much, the whirlwind trip to Memphis, when she had made a commitment to the man she loved more than life itself. She had gained her first true family member by marrying Thad Malone. Now, seeing her wedding anniversary coming up in the days ahead, Cassie decided to ask Dawn to accompany her to this place that had been so special to them.

"I can't think of anyone in my world who is more important than you, Treasa, and Drew. But with Carlton, they can't get away so easily. Would you consider going with me to Memphis?" Cassie asked.

"I would be so honored to share that place with you, knowing how much that weekend meant," Dawn said.

The two confirmed their plans, and Cassie began making the arrangements.

A bit of sadness overcame her as she realized that the last time she had made this trip, the elaborate plans had been made for her—and Thad. Money had been such an issue for them that she had never dreamed of such a trip for herself at the time. But that was no longer the case.

She was now financially secure, and for the first time realized the sadness in that as well. Cassie wanted to share this lifestyle with the love of her life. Tears of grief began to stream, something she had not allowed in so many years that she had thought maybe she had forgotten how to feel.

"I never realized how difficult it would be to take this trip without Thad. I have been thinking about him so much and wonder if he knew how much I truly loved him," she confessed to Larry in one of their nightly online chats, as Cassie told him of her plans.

He seemed genuinely excited, and replied by telling her to keep him posted along the journey. Larry confessed that he enjoyed their chats—and also had never concealed their correspondence from his wife. Cassie was relieved to find this out. Now, understanding that they were just friends, she hoped that his wife could see that too.

"She has always had the ability to read our chats. I've never kept my feelings from her, and I won't begin now. I do love her—even after all these years. My wife has always been and will continue to be my reason for living."

While his devotion to his wife sometimes left her longing for Thad that much more, Cassie wondered if this was one of the reasons she found Larry so easy to talk to. He was so much like the man she had remembered Thad to be. It was then that she realized that she had never been in love with Larry as much as with the idea of having what she'd lost when Thad died.

He had just brought out feelings that she had been choking back for so many years—feelings for her late husband. Cassie wished she had seen this originally.

Coming to terms with the fact that she couldn't have Thad, she had seen Larry as an easy substitute. Cassie now respected him as a friend and was happy to have him back in her life with no regrets about the nature of their relationship.

*C*assie knew that her baby, the foundation that she had built up from next to nothing, would be in good hands with Blu and Treasa at the helm. Her niece had been a very active part of the daily operations, and she had grown to rely on her so very much.

Once she finished packing for the airport, Cassie dialed her phone and then put her bags into the car. "I am on my way down to Memphis. I can't wait to see you there," she said excitedly as soon as Dawn's voicemail picked up the phone.

Dawn had been attending a meeting out of state, and the plans were for the two to meet up at the hotel later that day. As she listened to the voicemail message ringing out in her ear, she figured that Dawn was in flight. Cassie proceeded on with her plans, and within hours, she was pulling up to the entrance of the Peabody Hotel and was handing her keys to the valet as he unloaded her luggage from the trunk of the car.

She was filled with mixed emotions when she realized that she had been given the same room that she and Thad had shared years ago, and she was amazed to find that everything seemed to be the same as it had been then—even though so much else had changed in her life. Cassie was not nestling up to sleep in the arms of her beloved this time, and she suddenly realized that was harder to swallow than she thought it would be. Could she still be missing Thad so much? It actually took her by surprise—she thought her heart had healed from that loss. But she knew that she would overcome. She always did. Cassie was a strong woman—a survivor!

Much to her surprise, the room was filled with ros-es—everywhere she looked. She wondered if the hotel had made a mistake when they placed her in this room. It was so coincidental and brought about such painful mem-ories that she had blocked from her mind for so many years. Now they were right back in the forefront of her thoughts. Cassie reached for the phone, in an attempt to discuss the obvious mistake when she noticed a blink-ing light on the hotel phone. As she retrieved the mes-sage, her heart sank so deeply as Dawn's familiar voice informed her that she had gotten tied up with business and was unable to make the trip after all, but hoped that Cassie liked the surprises that had awaited her arrival.

Certain that Dawn had been misguided by attempting to recreate that special time for her, Cassie lay down on the beautifully rose-adorned bed and cried like she had done years ago when her loss was stingingly fresh. It was her wedding anniversary, and she was not only spending it without her groom, but she was going to be completely alone.

After she sobbed for an hour, her room phone rang. The concierge was calling, and before she could even get out the words to tell him about the room mix-up, he told her that friends had reserved a special seat to watch as the ducks marched back to the elevator later in the evening. This was not a request they generally accepted, but when they had been given the details of her trip by some very emphatic and influential friends, they'd felt obligated— even honored!

At this point, she realized that, while it was rather misguided, Dawn, Treasa and Drew thought she might like staying in that room. She wondered how they could have been so wrong about everything, and felt that the people closest to her must not really have known her at all.

The last thing Cassie wanted to do was to be surrounded by people, but she realized that at least one of her friends had gone to a lot of trouble, and felt that she owed it to whomever to put feelings aside. After all, how would she be able to face her well-meaning friend when she returned home if she didn't see this through?

She decided to open her laptop and attempt to chat with Larry for a while before heading downstairs. He always knew what to say to make her feel better. Once again, he acknowledged her chat but also said that he would not be able to talk for long as he had plans to meet his wife for dinner. Cassie was happy to get whatever time she could with him, and while her heart was still aching, she did feel better when the chat was over.

She checked in with the desk as instructed, in order to be escorted to her seat of honor. A roped-off section hosted a soft and comfy chair awaiting the arrival of an honored guest. Cassie felt like a dignitary or something— so far away from the orphan she had once been. She was not accustomed to such royal treatment. It had happened a couple of times in her lifetime, but she never had become comfortable with such attention.

She took her seat and began patiently waiting for the ducks to begin their parade to the elevator. Suddenly Cassie felt all eyes upon her as a well-dressed man appeared, and offered her a single red rose. There was a note attached to a small white satin bag. As she opened the bag, Cassie was overcome with emotion as she reached in and discovered that it contained her wedding ring. She had tucked it away in her jewelry box, inside the bag it had originally been presented in so many years before. Upon further inspection, she realized that it was in fact that very same white satin bag she had been handed one very special April morning.

At this point, confusion and anger began to seethe within her—someone was playing a cruel joke. She stood to walk out, not caring any longer about whether her family and friends had gone to trouble for her or not.

But just then, a pair of strong arms reached out from behind, and whirled her around. The face had aged a bit, but she could never mistake those baby blues. The voice was so familiar—she had heard it in her head so many times over the years. But the words that rang forth were completely unexpected.

"Hi, Cassie, I'm Larry. I've been waiting for this day for so long. I know that I have a lot to explain, but hope that, in time, you can find a way to forgive me."

At this point, feeling as though the earth itself had been pulled out from under her feet, much like she had felt when that 9-1-1 call had come in so many years ago, Cassie lost control of her emotions and fell toward the ground below.

But unlike the night of the 9-1-1 call, the arms she had longed for before were now catching her—keeping her from falling—giving that feeling of security once more.

So many things became clear to her as she thought back to the mysteries that had presented themselves during her years without Thad, but she also had many questions. At the same time, she found herself at a loss for words. Cassie stammered a bit and then gave up the idea of speaking at all.

"I know that you have questions, and I assure you, I have answers, and will share them with you all in good time. But for tonight, will you just accept that I never wanted to leave you? I truly hope that you will accept my dinner invitation and then let me hold you tightly for a while. I've missed you, my wife," Thad said.

She really didn't know how to feel about this new development. Cassie had dreamed about this day, but it angered her to think that he had made her suffer for so long. But at the same time, she had always trusted him, and that had not changed. Cassie was just glad to be back in his arms, realizing this was the one place she never dreamed she would ever be again.

The couple didn't hang around for the exit of the ducks. They just wanted to be alone together. Thad informed her that he'd had room service awaiting their return to the room. He had realized that she would need some time to process all of this.

Pieces began to fall into place, and Cassie began to put answers to her own questions. She felt some anger but realized that he must have had a good reason for leaving her. And now she was going to enjoy their anniversary—with him by her side! That realization far outweighed any negative emotions that might have been emerging.

As they entered the room and she spotted the room-service cart, Cassie realized that he had not forgotten her favorite foods: the cart contained almost all of them, right down to the Peabody Cheesecake for two.

Even considering all of the disappointment she had felt during the day, this was truly the best day of her life.

"You know that I love you still, but I do have more questions that you will have to answer in time. But for tonight, I just want to celebrate our love, a love that has proven to withstand the test of distance and time," said Cassie with a smile upon her somewhat aged face.

"I will tell you anything you want to know whenever you are ready to listen," he replied.

After dinner, Thad retired to his room. He knew that Cassie would need some time to come to terms with the events that had unfolded earlier that evening. But Cassie had found it impossible to sleep, knowing that Thad was in the next room. So she timidly knocked on his door, and asked if he would consider sitting up with her for the remained of the night.

She began with one simple but ever-so-important question. "I just need to know one thing. Are you back in my life, really?" Cassie was afraid to expect too much and worried that maybe he was just there as a temporary visitor. This had not crossed her mind in the excitement of the day before, but she'd had a bit of time to think now, and needed to know how to proceed.

"Yes, my love. I have no secrets. I will tell you everything in time, but just know that the reasons that took me from you have been resolved and I am with you now forever, if you will have me," he answered.

That wasn't even a question in her mind. Of course she would welcome him back into her life, even if it meant leaving the life she had built for herself.

He wasn't surprised to hear her response, since he had been anonymously keeping in touch with her over the years. At first she didn't really make the connection—but when he reminded her that he had been her chatting buddy, Larry, some of the questions were answered. Now she realized that it had been Thad doing the planning all along.

"I hope you don't mind, but I asked Dawn to back out of this trip after you told me about your plans in our chat that one night," he answered without her even asking. "I wanted to have this time alone with you, and when I called her last week, she informed me that she would have to leave town and stay away from you if I had any hopes of keeping this a secret until then. I also remembered that you had told me once, in a chat long ago, that you no longer wore your wedding ring, so I asked Dawn if she could send it to me."

Even more pieces—to a puzzle she had not realized existed—were now falling into place, and yet more were arising.

"I assured her that I would take good care of you. In fact, I let Dawn in on a few things, explaining to her that in many ways I always have. While your successes are clearly your own, and I would never take that away from you, I do want you to realize that I've watched you grow from afar—and helped when I could."

Suddenly one question became clear to her. "You know Dawn?" she asked. "I am sure that I may have mentioned her over the years of our chats, but how on earth did you find out how to get in touch with her?"

"Sweetheart, Dawn has been a true friend to you over the years, and first of all, I never want you to doubt that fact," Thad answered. "That is all part of the story I have to tell you. But please just share some time with me, enjoying one another. We have a lifetime to talk about the rest."

This made Cassie wonder how much he had done for her. Why had he not come back to her sooner? What reasons could he have possibly had for making her suffer like she had? She realized that she did need a few answers now, and he obliged her request. The two sat in the solitude and extravagance that the room offered and just talked.

She began at the beginning—the moment his truck had crashed down into the ravine. "Were you injured? Amnesia? What happened?" Things weren't making much sense. Assuming that he had been injured, maybe suffering a concussion and possible amnesia, why hadn't he come back to her after he'd regained his memory? At one point, Cassie realized that she had fired out so many questions that he would never be able to answer them all in even a day's time. She apologized and then asked him to just start at the beginning and tell her what happened on that day—if he could remember.

"Of course I remember, Cassie," he began. "What you don't realize is that I was not in my rig when it burned. That part of the accident was staged. In order to keep you safe, I had to do what I was told. Understand that I was not given a chance to tell you, but did try to assure you whenever I could that I was still part of your world. I witnessed something just after leaving work that night that left me with very few options."

Cassie had tears in her eyes as she listened to his words, now realizing what he had been forced to do to the life they had built together. "What did you witness, love?" she asked.

"It had been such a typical day up until my routine stop at the Stover Plaza. I walked out with my daily cookie and coke, and was climbing back into my cab when I heard a disturbance from across the parking lot. Just as I was about to jump down and inform the girls inside, I heard gunshots and realized that I just needed to get away. Three men, having heard my truck, jumped into a nearby car and chased after me. I watched in my rear view mirror and noticed that car was losing speed, and they were unable to keep up. I just wanted to get done with my trip and return home to you so I kept driving. Though I tried to proceed with my night as though nothing had happened, the sight of flashing lights in my rear view mirror, as I approached the 110 mile-marker, soon changed my world—our world. As the unmarked cars lined up behind me, I realized that this was not just your typical traffic stop."

Cassie's tears were now flowing abundantly, and Thad wondered if he should stop telling his story for now, but continued upon her insistence.

"I later found out that the man who was murdered had been scheduled to testify against the Garringer family. They had been involved in a huge drug ring and the head of the family had ordered this man killed. When the federal agents caught up to me that day, they told me that there would undoubtedly be a contract out on my life now as well. They told me that they were going to stage my death and then hide me until I could testify against the family. I agreed, thinking that you would be told and I would be allowed to return to our lives in a matter of weeks. I was so wrong! I want you to know that it was never my decision to leave you. But I knew that if I didn't follow their instructions, I would be putting your life in great danger. I couldn't allow that to happen, no matter what," Thad said. "They placed me into one of the cars that had lined up behind my trailer and informed me that you would be taken care of in the best way possible".

"I did ask them for a few favors initially and promised to do whatever they asked as long as they would allow me the opportunity to make your pain lessen. They advised me to proceed with caution, and I was never again permitted to contact you, though they did honor my one request—to allow me a brief stop at our home while you attended the memorial service that you had planned for me."

"I placed a note inside our anniversary clock when my handler turned her back for a moment. I hoped that you would find it when you noticed that the clock had stopped."

"Thad, I never found the note because I just couldn't bear the silence that seemed to echo from the stationary hands on the face of the clock. It was as though they were taunting me—that time meant nothing now. I haven't even bothered to look at it since that day. It just hurt too much," Cassie retorted.

"Oh, baby, I am so sorry that my attempt to comfort you added grief to your already stressed situation. I really thought that I was making things better, or I would have never done it. I wanted to tell you that no matter what the days, weeks, and months ahead held for you, I was never going to be far away. I wanted to assure you that our love would withstand any obstacle, and had hoped that you would find it and think that I had put it in there at some time during our years together. I guess it was dumb of me to assume, but I was desperate to ease the pain I knew that you would be feeling. I never doubted the depth of your love for me and knew that it would be very difficult for you to go on without me, but I had no idea that I would have to stay away for so long. I had to testify in the major federal case and was naive enough to think that once I upheld my civic duty I would be returned to you. That was not the case, and my main goal had to be to keep you safe," Thad explained.

Cassie thought back and wondered what else he had done during this brief stop.

With that, Thad reached into his luggage and pulled out something that made Cassie's already leaking eyes flow even more. "Here is something else that I took on that day when I put the note inside the clock," he said. He was holding in his hand that very same frame that held the picture taken at the moment when they had become husband and wife, the first time they had visited Memphis together. "I also took this. I am sorry, but I needed something to hold close to me in your absence, and it was the first thing I saw," he continued.

"I still wanted you to have a life, to have comfort. There were two federal agents left in charge of my safety—a man and a woman. While my pleas to help you fell upon deaf ears with the man, the woman found a way to oblige. Agent Spears told me that she was getting ready to retire and intended to do whatever she could to minimize your pain, so she bought a ticket to board a plane from North Carolina and found an empty seat next to you."

Cassie nodded. So it had not been fate that had brought Dawn to her, but Thad—and Dawn herself.

There were many details he didn't share, like when the evil men had realized that the accident was staged, found the safe house where he had awaited his new identity, and made an attempt on his life. While Cassie was sad to hear that he had gone through so much, she was finding comfort in the knowledge that he had never meant to leave her. "So you created Larry?" she asked.

"Yes Cassie. I remembered a story you told me once of an imaginary friend who made you feel safe during your years growing up in the orphanage. I had hoped that the association of the name would offer you comfort at times. I knew that we could not meet, back when you made the request a few years ago—it was still not safe then, and it broke my heart when you let me go," he sobbed.

"Oh my God, Thad, I am so very sorry. If I'd only known. But I was so hurt when you told me that you had a wife. Does that mean that you are remarried?" she asked sadly.

"Oh no, my love," he emphatically replied. "You are my wife. From that my mind never strayed. When I told you that I have a wife whom I love with all of my heart, it was you that I was speaking of. I just couldn't tell you that part. I knew that it would hurt for a while, but I had also witnessed great strength in you as I saw where your life had taken you over the years, and my main priority was always to keep you safe. I even spotted you in a crowd once and hoped that you had not seen me. I just had to see things for myself—had to know that you were really as okay as they were telling me." Thad paused and smiled. "In fact, I had to let you know that you were loved and remembered, especially on Valentine's Day. Once I even found a way to send you flowers. It was the year after you turned away from our chats. I was worried about you and wanted to put a smile upon your face."

Cassie laughed. "I freaked out when I saw them as I returned home that day. I tried to find out who had sent them to me. I actually suspected 'Larry' initially but discounted him when I realized that I had never given him my address. Of course, you were never a consideration. I really felt that someone was playing a sick joke on me since you were the only person who would have known just how special those particular flowers were to me. They were the same flowers I held when I took your name. Oh, and by the way, I hope you don't think bad of me that I did try to find love again.

But I could never seem to make it work. I realized that I was trying to replace you in them, and I finally just stopped trying."

Thad assured her that he had never expected her to stop living. After all, she had thought that he was dead. "I am okay with everything you did when I was gone from your life. It is very important that you know that, Cassie. I have always loved you and wanted what was best for you. And I want you to realize that I am extremely proud of everything you have accomplished. You should be proud of yourself as well," he said.

Suddenly, the two realized that the sun was beginning to set—it was the first time they'd peered through the curtains to notice the sky at all that day. Cassie and Thad had literally spent the day just talking. But it was no surprise. After all, they had years to catch up on—and now the rest of their lives to do just that.

They decided it was time to take a break from the overwhelmingly emotional day they had been sharing so far, and chose to hold off any further discussion for the time being. Cassie and Thad vacated the room in search of nourishment.

After a quick dinner, they decided to return to her hotel room for a quiet evening together—alone.

Cassie knew that she would forgive Thad for anything, and the answers he had given her thus far had put many of her questions to rest already. She laid her head upon his shoulder. She'd forgotten how much she truly missed how it felt.

She spent that night wrapped tightly in the arms she had longed to feel for what seemed an eternity. Cassie had grown to realize that the love she had felt so long ago would never be an option for her again. After all, a love like hers and Thad's comes along only once in a lifetime. She knew this to be true still as she realized that their love had never died. It had been a big part of her life—even in his absence. She had recognized that her decisions over the years had been based a lot on what he would have wanted for her.

Cassie awoke several times during the night to something so familiar, yet strange. The snoring of her one true love was such a welcomed sound. She had missed it so much when he'd disappeared from her bed all those years ago and had realized that if she ever got the chance to hear it again, she would be much more accepting. She had done a lot of soul searching in the early days of her grieving process and realized that his snores meant he was comfortable with her by his side. He would only snore when she lay next to him, and at one time, she'd suspected that he was somehow just doing it to annoy her on a subconscious level. Grief had given her the opportunity to view things with a new perspective—a perspective that even time couldn't take.

Even though she had woken up several times during the night, when Cassie opened her eyes that next morning, she felt fully rested—something she had not felt in years. After everything she had accomplished in her life since Thad had departed from her world, she had never felt as complete as she felt in this moment. She had never doubted what had been missing during those years, and never thought that she would feel this way again.

Thad opened his eyes, and she was so relieved to be staring once more into those baby blues. Although an ocean view had come close once, his eyes were a color she had forgotten since she had been unable to find it anywhere else in her world—once he had gone.

Once they finished a quick breakfast, they hopped on board for a reminiscent trolley ride.

She listened as he declared his love for her. "Cassie, you know that I love you so very much. These past several years have been extremely difficult for me as well, but I intend to spend the rest of my days proving my love to you. I felt that I had no choice, and you were always in my heart."

Cassie, now able to relax in the one place she had longed to be for so many years, closed her eyes as the trolley trundled through the streets of Memphis. Thad leaned in and kissed her forehead as he repeated once more, "Remember, I promised to love you forever—and that's a promise I intend to keep. Cassie, you are *forever loved*!"

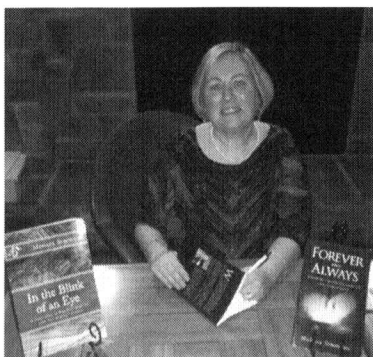

About the Author

Melissa Heepke-Simmons was raised on a small dairy farm in Illinois. She currently lives in a quaint little tourist town along the Mississippi River. A college graduate who earned her associate's degree in computer programming, she has worked in a variety of occupations, including real estate and roadside work for a car rental company.

After the heartbreaking loss of her husband of twenty-three years, Heepke-Simmons decided to turn her focus to writing in order to fulfill his dream for her.

A proud mother and grandmother, she is also the author of three books: *Forever and Always*, *In the Blink of an Eye*, and *Forever Loved*.